SPLINTERED SHADOW

SHATTERED GALAXIES

NANCEY CUMMINGS

ABOUT SPLINTERED SHADOW

The portals take...

So I forgot to update my phone. Big deal. Only there's a glitch and an app opens a portal to another planet! Because that makes sense.

Now I'm stuck on an alien planet with a grumpy prince. His eyes turn black when he's upset. He can manipulate the shadows and grow a pair of massive inky wings. I mean, sure, he's hot, and he saved me from a pack of monsters, but I don't trust anything about this place, let alone a surly alien.

I'm going to find a way home.

The portals give...

Fate delivered this odd, soft female to me. The royal mark is inked into her skin. She is meant for greatness. Then why did I, the half-blind prince, find her?

Now that I have her, I refuse to let her go. She is my fate, my mate, and my destiny.

SHATTERED GALAXIES

When an elite group of scientists cracked the code on a special artificial intelligence, it began to understand emotion and the mechanics to maintain itself. An AI as close to a human as humanly possible.

It was a mistake.

With unmeasured reach, it searched for other life-forms, hoping to expand its knowledge about the universe beyond the boundaries its creators established.

The scientists shut it down before it could spiral into something they couldn't stop. The group went silent, shutting themselves off from the public as they set out to rebuild, hoping to regain control over their greatest creation.

The world moved on, the possibility of a special AI once more reserved for science fiction.

Until a year later, when it all went wrong.

CHAPTER ONE

SARAH

ANOTHER END TO A LONG DAY.

The silence of the empty apartment greeted Sarah as she dumped her bag and keys at the table next to the front door. Working at a bookstore sounded great—plenty of things to read and new stock arriving daily—and it would be if it weren't for all the customers.

I want the book they talked about on the radio. No clue about the name or even what program they heard it on.

It was on the radio, the customer repeated, like it should be obvious.

Or, a perennial favorite, *I'm looking for a book. It's blue.*

Customers were the absolute worst.

Sarah wanted a shower, and then she wanted to stuff her face with something unhealthy. The day had worn her out. Her feet hurt, and her patience was long since gone, but the laundry demanded to be done. She wore her last clean pair of underwear, and there was no chance of wearing the same work shirt tomorrow.

Sarah frowned down at the barbeque sauce stain gracing the front of her unflattering polo.

Yup. Laundry had to be done. Such a glamorous life she led.

After a quick shower, she ran the first load and finished the leftover mac and cheese in the fridge. She caught up on the latest episodes of a baking competition while the laundry ran.

The phone chirped, reminding her of an important system update.

"They're all important," she grumbled and dismissed the message. She should update, but the last time she tried, it demanded to be plugged into the charger, and the charger was all the way in the bedroom.

Sarah imagined getting off the comfy couch and just couldn't find it in her. "Tomorrow," she promised.

She carried the basket into her bedroom. "No, I'm tired. I'll fold you tomorrow," she said.

The basket had heard that before.

She sighed and dumped the basket out on the bed. "Fine, I'll be an adult, but I'm not happy about this. Some people have those things, whatsits, *friends*, and a life. I should get one of those."

She had friends, but most were partnered up and having babies. Everyone was too busy or too tired to hang out. Honestly, now that she approached her thirties, leaving the apartment after work just seemed like a waste of energy. Adulting was no joke.

She popped in her earbuds, cued up an audiobook, and set to folding. Losing herself in the narrator's voice, she matched socks and folded shirts.

The phone vibrated.

"David has the baby. Let's get an adult beverage!"

Sarah smiled at Trisha's message. *"Can't,"* she replied.

"OMG, that means you're sitting at home in your underwear."

"I'm wearing pants!" For some inexplicable reason.

"You're so old."

Sarah checked the time and did the math. She lived on the other side of the city from Trisha. With driving time and the fact that Trisha would insist on coffee and then a late-night cheesesteak, she'd be out all night.

"I have to open tomorrow," Sarah wrote.

The reply came instantly. *"Poo. I hate that you live so far away now."*

Sarah sucked in her breath. Her friends knew why she moved, even though no one talked about it.

Three bouncing dots appeared on the screen.

"Sorry. I suck. Don't be mad. I just miss you," Trisha wrote.

And Sarah missed Robert. Three years after her fiancé's unexpected death from an aneurysm, it still hurt. One day he had a headache, laid down for a nap, and never woke up.

The grief counselor told her not to make any big changes right away, but Sarah couldn't sleep in the same bed—their bed. Staying in the same apartment was too much. She felt stuck in molasses, sunken by the memories, and needed to break free. So she moved as far as she could to keep a reasonable commute to her job. On a good traffic day, it was an hour's drive to the old neighborhood, her friends, and her parents' house. Close, but not too close.

It was great. New grocery store. New gas station. No memories waiting to ambush her every time she passed their Sunday morning bagel place. No neighbors with concerned frowns asking her how she was doing.

It was also lonely.

The apartment seemed even emptier, just her and the laundry basket.

Robert wouldn't want her holed up in her apartment, hiding behind the excuse of laundry and work to avoid people. He'd want her to go out and enjoy herself. Live.

Re-engage with the community, the grief counselor called it. They wrote the phrase down on Sarah's action plan like those were steps she would actually take before their next appointment.

She sighed and picked up the phone. *"Give me an hour. I need to put on my face."*

Trisha replied with a series of emojis that made no sense.

Star. Peach. Exclamation point. Lightning bolt. Dog. Heart. Heart.

"See you soon," Trisha wrote.

Her chest tightened, panicking at the audacity of her *going out* and *having fun* with friends.

"Dammit," she muttered, blinking quickly to avoid crying. She tossed the phone down, swiping at her eyes. This wasn't a big deal. This was doing things she used to enjoy with people she liked. This was part of her action plan.

Her phone buzzed and vibrated next to her on the bed.

"Trisha, not now." She was hurrying as fast as she could and not in the mood to be teased about being a slow poke.

The power went off in the building. The only light came from the phone's screen.

Color swirled and pulsed across the screen.

"Initiating..." The words flashed across the screen.

Light erupted from the phone, swirling above the bed. Red, blue, yellow… a rainbow-colored vortex materialized. The air pressure dropped. Sarah felt it in her bones. Then a sudden *whoosh* as the vortex sucked everything toward it.

This was not good.

Sarah scrambled back. Hair whipped around her face. Clothes—socks, tops, the slippers on her feet—were pulled into the swirling rainbow portal.

It caught her ankle. The force of it yanked her leg up and sent her flat to her back.

Sarah flopped over, clutching the mattress. Blankets and sheets came away, flying up to partially cover her face, and she was dragged through the vortex.

VEKELE

"An anomaly," Vekele said.

He tilted his head to better view the information on the tablet's screen. An anomaly could be anything from a sensor malfunction to interference from a solar flare.

Or an invading force trying to slip through Arcos' security.

"An anomaly," Baris agreed.

The karu perched on top of a bookshelf ruffled her inky black feathers. She did not like this. Neither did he. Baris had been assigning Vekele tasks—all meaningless—to give him purpose.

Vekele did not need his brother's pity. He was perfectly content on the isolated country estate, away from court.

Nothing good ever happened in the palace.

"It is a malfunctioning sensor," Vekele said, handing the tablet back to his brother.

"I would hardly send you to chase after a bit of space dust. Investigate the anomaly." Baris spoke with an air of authority, as a male who was seldom questioned. Too many people bowed and scraped for Baris' favor, in Vekele's opinion. Bootlickers and worse.

Fortunately, Vekele had no difficulties questioning his brother, king of Arcos or not.

"I am no longer a soldier," he said, waving a hand to crowded shelves and the table piled high with ancient books. After the attack that damaged his eyes and cost him his position in the military, Vekele retreated to the country estate and surrounded himself with tomes of military history. "Who needs one who is half-blind?"

"Exactly, and they say you're not the smart one," Baris said.

The karu cawed and clicked, unimpressed by Baris' wit.

His brother glanced up at the massive bird. His four eyes blinked—two in the front and then the two at the side—in apology.

This appeased the karu. Vekele felt a warm flush of appreciation for his companion. She had always been protective of him. Why she had chosen him, being ancient and powerful, he never understood.

The karu—average size for an adult—on Baris' shoulders cawed in reply. The tone sounded offended, but whatever the karu felt—offense, annoyance at the lack of deference—Baris kept that to himself.

Baris pushed the tablet to Vekele. "It is unusual. The analysts have failed to identify the energy signature, and I cannot send a ship to investigate."

"Because of the wedding," Vekele said.

"Because any military movement would be seen as aggressive and would put a halt to the treaty. We need this treaty," Baris said.

Politics.

Vekele had no stomach for the intricate webs spun at court. Motives. Plots within plots. Blackmail. Betrayal. Spies.

Spies were vermin, always there, sniffing after crumbs.

He much preferred a straightforward approach. No one would ever accuse the king's brother of subtlety. Baris had a mind for political maneuvering. Vekele was better suited for the battlefield and perfectly content to follow his king's orders.

You were *better suited.*

Vekele resisted the urge to flinch at his thoughts and kept his expression blank. He loathed pity, especially his own. Pity did nothing. He said, "Sending the king's brother off on a mission would draw as much attention."

"Fortunately, the king's brother is known to be recovering from his injuries. No one will blink twice at a meditative retreat to the temples of Miria."

"The anomaly is at Miria?"

Interesting. A sacred location, various myths surrounded Miria. Superstitious nonsense, in Vekele's opinion, but now this anomaly…perhaps the myths had a basis in reality.

"Ah, you are intrigued. It is decided." Baris nodded at his words. "Take Kenth, my personal ship, and as many guards as Kenth feels are needed. Yes?" Baris directed this question to the female guard lurking just outside the doorway of the library. The head of the royal guard never strayed far from Baris.

"I will handle it," Kenth said.

Vekele found Kenth to be very capable if lacking in subtlety. There was no such thing as too many weapons or too many guards. "Perhaps only one or two guards," he suggested. "I am an injured male seeking solitude, after all. Too much security will draw attention."

Kenth nodded in agreement.

Baris clapped Vekele on the shoulder. "I need your eyes on this."

Heat flushed over Vekele. Any mention of his eyes was usually followed by an insult.

Half-blind prince.

"If I find an enemy incursion?" Vekele asked.

"Do not engage. Return to the inner zone. You are too important to lose."

"But not too important to risk on reconnaissance." Vekele tilted his head to better look at his brother. Was this a ploy to send the family's disgrace away on a fool's errand? Or to eliminate a rival to the throne?

No. For all Baris' faults—ego, hubris, a stunning lack of modesty—he had never treated Vekele as a disgrace or less than capable. And Vekele did not want the throne. He never had. Still, he had no idea what poison councilors whispered in Baris' ear. They might convince

Baris that Vekele's continued existence was a threat to the stability of his reign.

In darker moments, Vekele had wondered if Baris ordered the attack that blinded him. A ruined soldier could not rally forces to his side and seize the throne. Such treachery among the royal family had happened within living memory. The fact was, Vekele had been a popular military figure with success on the battlefield. Many of the nobles only considered the king to be strong if that strength was delivered with bloodshed.

A shortsighted opinion, in Vekele's mind.

Arcos had been torn apart for decades by civil war. As various noble houses gambled to seize the throne, Arcos grew more and more isolated from the rest of the galaxy. Once they had thriving trade. Now they had an abandoned station in orbit. Once Arcos boasted the most respected warriors in the quadrant with an extensive fleet of starships. Now the fleet had been reduced to a handful of ships that could barely break the atmosphere.

The planet needed peace, and Baris had the cunning and the determination to forge peace from the broken shards of the past. Those who regarded Baris as weak were fools. Baris felt the weight of the crown. Vekele did not envy the difficult decisions his brother had to make.

Was blinding him one of those decisions?

Vekele did not want to believe it.

The karu on Baris' shoulder clicked his beak in an agitated manner. Baris soothed the creature with a few strokes on the head.

"There are many pieces on the game board at the moment. An anomaly amid treaty negotiations is suspicious. Responding in any way feels like an error, but doing nothing also feels wrong," Baris said, planting his hands on the table. Next to his fingers, a pair of children had long ago carved their initials into the wood.

B.S.

V.S.

Baris ran his thumb over the carving. "I do not know how you can tolerate this place. It is a prison."

A luxurious prison with ten bedrooms, a library, a study, a drawing room, formal and informal dining rooms, a room for sitting in the morning, a room just for eating breakfast, a kitchen so enormous it required a small army to operate, extensive gardens, undisturbed hunting grounds, and a stable.

"Our time here never bothered me," Vekele said. He had been ten when their uncle took them into protective custody at the country house. To a youthful, unjaded Vekele, the guards were friends and not prison wardens. He had missed his parents and his friends from the capital, but the grounds offered much in the way of distraction to an energetic child.

It was only as he grew older that he understood what the golden band on his ankle meant, what his scheming uncle had taken from him and his brother.

"I suppose I have you to thank for that. You always took care of me," he said.

"Come back to the palace," Baris replied.

"Is that a command, Your Majesty?"

The king positioned his hand over the carved initials, splaying it wide, as if to obscure the past. "Not yet. Must it be?"

"Not yet," Vekele replied. He scratched the back of his neck, knowing he needed to give in to his brother's request. Baris would not cease until he had his way. He said, "Even if this anomaly is a bit of dust, the trip to Miria will be worthwhile."

Miria. The location where the first karu bonded with an Arcosian, where his people's history began.

Where our parents' lives ended.

Baris gave a victorious shout and pulled Vekele into a powerful embrace. "Return home safely. Bring me something interesting."

After the king and his guard left, the library felt empty.

Baris needed him.

After the attack, Vekele had retreated to his books and maps. He made himself as unthreatening as possible, a broken male studying the great battles of the past. No one particularly cared for Arcos' distant history. His preference was to be ignored so he could get along with his studies, but the king gave him a task. His brother needed him. He would bring the same discipline and demand for perfection to this as he did to his research. He would find this anomaly, be it an incursion or an entire invading army.

The karu fluttered down from the bookshelf, landing on the table. Papers scattered.

"Those are delicate," he said.

The karu squawked, feathers puffed up. She was unhappy. Their connection did not allow for words but gave him impressions. Curious or furious, Vekele knew her opinion on matters.

"Yes, I agree, but we have no choice," Vekele said. If Baris saw Vekele as a threat to the stability of his reign and wanted that threat removed, there were easier ways than a convoluted mission to a sacred temple. "We must obey our king."

If it were a trap, he would know soon enough.

CHAPTER TWO

SARAH

A BUZZING WOKE HER. More like birdsong. Angry birdsong.

Her head throbbed. Harsh sunlight just made it worse. Hot and sticky, the humidity must have arrived overnight. May was like that. One day was rainy and cool, the next was all sweaty. Spring was over. Time to swelter in the summer heat.

Sarah groaned, shielding her eyes from the sun. Turning her head, nausea rolled over her.

Big mistake.

What was this? How many drinks did she have with Trisha? And since when did her alarm sound like a bird trying to deep throat a jackhammer? Chirpy and mechanical and so freaking *loud*.

Awareness trickled in. Her bed didn't just feel like the ground, it was the ground.

She cracked open an eye.

A vivid blue sky stretched over her. She wasn't sure the exact shade—azure dreams, tropical waters, something unreal and more likely to be found on a paint swatch than in real life, certainly not in Philadelphia.

Oh, and the two moons huddled next to the sun in the sky. That was new.

Sarah carefully rolled to her side and picked herself up. Stone scraped the palms of her hands. Dirt and plant matter covered the surface. Tufts of grass and twisting, flowering vines covered the area, along with her bedsheets and scattered socks. Narrow trumpet-shaped flowers reached for the sun, the outside petals violet, and the interior a vivid orange.

Using her hand to shield her eyes against the sunlight, she slowly surveyed the scene.

She definitely wasn't in Philadelphia anymore.

A thick green forest surrounded her on three sides.

A large stone building loomed behind her. Rectangular tiers were stacked atop one another. Plant life seemed to swallow up the building at the base. Cream-colored stone burst free of the thick growth, but the weather had taken a toll.

Ruins, she realized. She was looking at ruins.

She was currently sitting on the flat top of a stone pyramid. Peering over the edge confirmed the existence of steps, but doing so made her stomach flip.

Not going to tackle those for a while.

Sarah just knew she would grow dizzy and tumble down the endless flight of stone steps. Just being this close to the edge made her nervous. She shuffled back, scooting her butt on the ground.

Her hand brushed against her phone. She remembered the strange warning and the swirling thing that opened above the phone. A portal? A wormhole? Something fucky. The whole situation was fucky, and Sarah wished she had paid more attention to the science fiction books at the store.

Twin moons hung in the sky, pale orbs in the daylight and unavoidable, watching her like… some metaphor or shit.

Fuck if she knew. She was never any good at metaphors. Staring directly at them gave her a sense of vertigo, like she was falling off the… wherever she was. Roof? If this was an alien sky and not a hallucination brought on by food poisoning from dodgy mac and cheese, then she had to be on a planet.

Although a hallucination made more sense. Some plants, like jimsonweed, caused intense visions. Jimsonweed had tubular white flowers.

Sarah eyed the violet and orange tubular flowers surrounding her. She didn't know exactly how she came to consume the seeds of jimsonweed—or any hallucinogen—but it happened all the time in the murder mysteries she read. You could never trust a baked good from a neighbor with a grudge or accept a drink at a party unless you wanted to be dead.

She ran a finger along the nearest vine leaf, surprised to find it rough. Knowing her red herrings from legitimate clues wouldn't help her now.

She really should have read more sci-fi.

Reaching for her phone, she checked for a signal out of habit. It didn't make sense to her, either. A body just moved on autopilot when overwhelmed, which was why Sarah stretched her hand up to raise the phone, like that would get a better signal.

A crack spread across the screen, either from the trip through the portal or the fall. She squeezed the phone in frustration. She resisted the urge to throw it because if this was a hallucination, she didn't want to wake up in her bedroom with a busted phone. Those things were expensive. Instead, she tucked it into her bra on the side near the strap.

Nothing felt real. Not the sunlight. Not the birdsong from the trees. Nothing except her killer headache.

So she waited. Sweating. Itching from where the strange vines rubbed against her skin, leaving red welts.

"Great. I'm allergic," she muttered. Her throat felt dry and sitting in the sun was not doing her head any favors.

Sarah hauled herself to her feet—no shoes, because of course not. The dizziness wasn't so bad. She took a step, gasping at how wrong it felt, like the ground was made of the rubberized playground material. Was that gravity, or was the stone different? No, it felt like stone when she had her face pressed up against it. Her body ached like it landed on stone.

She bounced on her toes, testing gravity. Yup, it was lighter. Not Earth or a strangely specific hallucination.

Bare feet picked her way through the vines. She felt filthy and didn't want to think of all the cuts and scrapes on her poor feet. Where had her slippers gone? They went through the vortex, too, but were now missing along with most of her laundry. Speaking of…

Sarah reached down to grab a sock, the blue one with an orange octopus.

The ground gave way. Screaming, she grabbed onto a vine, the rough leaves sliding through her hands as she fell.

Finally, she stopped, twisted in vines, and dangling in midair. The vines creaked alarmingly when she moved.

Sarah grabbed hold and attempted to pull herself up. Easier said than done. Flashbacks of third -grade gym class played in her mind as little Sarah tried to pull herself up the rope.

Who had the upper arm strength to do that?

Another creak.

The vines snapped, and she fell.

VEKELE

"Are we even allowed to be on Miria?" Luca asked. "This place is too rarified for my blood."

"Miria is sacred, not prohibited," Vekele said. Travel to and from the mountain was controlled to maintain the fragile ecosystem. Colonies of karu existed elsewhere on Arcos, but this region was the ancestral home of the creatures.

"For a royal," Luca said.

Vekele tilted his head, staring at the male from a good angle. A round face gave the appearance of youth. A foolhardy person would dismiss the male as benign, but he was a member of the royal guard, therefore dangerous.

He resisted the urge to ask if the male spoke to his king in such a manner, but Vekele knew the answer. While Vekele never tolerated insubordinate behavior when he was a Revenant, Baris actively encouraged it.

The male had the good sense to appear shamefaced.

"Visiting is simply a matter of applying for a permit. Royal or not," Vekele said in a tone that discouraged further conversation.

Kenth made a noncommittal grunting noise, her contribution to the conversation.

"Scans indicate an unidentified life form," Luca said.

Vekele brought up a surface map of the terrain. Twin red dots indicated the location of the anomaly and the life form. Both were too close to the temple complex for his liking.

"Land here," he said, jabbing the holo with a finger.

"We can get closer to the location of the anomaly," Luca said.

"We are capable of walking. It is best not to disturb the karu." This was a deception, though the creatures nested in the temple complex. Distressing the karu invited misfortune. Vekele was not a superstitious male, but if Luca questioned his reasoning, he would admit to not wanting to upset the sacred creatures, just in case.

He had enough misfortune for a lifetime.

In truth, he did not want to see the landing site, any part of it. The scorch marks and blood were long gone after twenty years, but they remained fresh in his mind.

Once the ship landed, his karu settled on his shoulder. Talons dug into the feather mantle on his shoulders, but he felt the sharp pang in his skin.

Anticipation zipped through him. Vekele could not say why. Yes, as they arrived on Miria, it became apparent that an anomaly had occurred. Strange energy signatures lingered.

Not a bit of space dust on a sensor, then.

But investigating a genuine anomaly could not explain why he felt as if he were on the cusp of some great change. The last time he felt this way had been the choosing ceremony when he reached the age of ten.

His parents had acted strangely in the weeks leading up to the event. Baris had taken the same journey to Miria, made an offering of salt and blood, and bonded with a karu. It was a rite of passage taken by every member of the Shadowmark family.

On the day, an uneasiness permeated the atmosphere. What was normally a celebration on a child's tenth birthday was done three days early and in secrecy.

His parents had worn empty smiles, poorly hiding their worry. It was a dangerous time to leave the safety of the capital, though young Vekele did not understand this at the time. He worried he would not be chosen and feared disappointing his parents.

As it happened, Vekele did not have to worry about his parents' disappointment.

The karu nipped his ear, drawing his attention to the present.

"I need to be mindful," he said, raising a hand to stroke the karu's head. She leaned into his touch, cooing softly.

Despite their worry, they brought him to the temple. Baris had been chosen almost as soon as he set foot in the temple. A karu swooped down and started chattering, as if asking Baris what took him so long. They knew the same would be true with Vekele. With an embrace, his mother told him to be quick and that they would wait for him outside.

He had not been quick.

He kneeled at the ancient altar, made the offering, and waited.

And waited.

The light vanished, and he waited through the freezing hours of night. Doubt crept in. The ceremony lasted until dawn, but his family had always been chosen. The only member of the royal family not to be chosen was Rasat the Cruel, a prince so reviled that his image had been removed from the archives. Young Vekele had researched all this to ease his worries.

It had not worked. Rather than be ignorant of the ceremony, of the history that tied his family to the symbiotic relationship with the karu, of the parasite that tied them together, he had found the forbidden family history that no one spoke of.

As the night stretched on, Vekele knew his name would be stricken from the family histories. He was nothing but a source of shame, which was far too heavy a burden for a child.

His fears had been for naught. In the moments before dawn, his karu arrived. Ancient and massive, she landed on his back, knocking him down to the ground. Chirping happily, she immediately preened his hair, like an untidy child.

When he emerged from the temple, he discovered the slaughtered remains of his parents and their guard.

While they waited, exposed outside the safety of the palace, his uncle seized the opportunity and the crown. Baris and Vekele had been imprisoned at the remote estate for "their safety" until Baris was old enough to rule. Until then, their uncle acted as regent.

Rage still burned inside him for the cruelty and the betrayal.

Vekele shook away old memories. They helped no one.

The karu flexed her wings and dug her talons into his shoulder before launching herself into the sky. She soared, her cries in the wind, and headed for the top of the central temple.

"The life form is on the move," Luca said, gesturing with a scanner in hand.

Kenth drew her weapon. "Approach silently," she said, motioning for Luca to move ahead. "Stay back, Your Highness."

Vekele's temper ruffled at the female's command but held his tongue. Kenth was the captain of the royal guard, and Vekele was no longer a commanding officer.

Focus on the mission. He would have time enough to brood over all he lost in the last year.

They moved silently through the grass as they approached the temple complex. No trace remained of the betrayal that took his parents. He knew this, but a childish fear had lingered, that the grass would still be red with their blood.

Focus. Baris gave you a mission. Prove that you are still useful to your king.

The temple appeared much the same, despite the vegetation. There had been snow on the ground at the time of his ceremony.

He couldn't imagine a spy infiltrating a karu sanctuary, sacred or not, but a saboteur...yes. That would put an end to the treaty negotiations. They needed to intercept the individual before any damage could be done.

A female's scream pierced the silence.

SARAH

Today was the worst.

The fall knocked the breath out of her. She lay gasping, willing herself to breathe evenly instead of gulping erratically. The world eventually stopped spinning, and she sat upright.

Sarah carefully touched her head, dismayed to feel wetness. Amazingly, she still had the octopus sock clutched in one hand. She pressed the sock to her head to stop the bleeding. Touching the wound hurt, but, honestly, her wrist hurt worse. It took her weight when she landed and had to be sprained.

Wherever she was, it was dark and stifling. Sweat crawled down her skin, making her itch. Still, this was marginally better than baking under an alien sun.

And it was an alien sun. Sarah knew this in her gut. Call it dream logic, where you just know. The sun, the sky, even the vines... they had been familiar, but just off enough to remind her she wasn't on Earth. Not plunging to her certain demise was also a big clue. She landed hard, but not as hard as she would have had she fallen through a roof onto a stone floor.

At least on Earth.

The fall knocked the breath out of her, but she should have broken bones, something more than a wrist that smarted and a scrape on her head.

That portal transported her to another world.

Sunlight filtered through the hole in the ceiling. The vines swayed, moved by an air current. Shafts of sunlight pierced the darkness at regular intervals, making Sarah believe that a giant hole in the roof was a design choice and not structural failure.

Pillars formed a ring around her. The vines cast shadows. As the vines moved with the breeze, the shadows shifted. In the distance, she heard splashing water.

Groaning, she hauled herself to her feet. Everything ached, and there would be a hell of a bruise on her butt tomorrow, but hey, her useless phone was still snug in her bra. So success?

Sarah pulled out the phone, dismayed to see the cracked screen and the power at less than twenty-five percent. In a fit of optimism that maybe her phone would do that portal thing again and she could go home, she put it to sleep to conserve juice.

The phone went back into the bra. What now? She needed to think, and if her head would stop spinning, that'd be fantastic.

She limped toward the nearest pillar. It was covered in symbols carved into the stone. Was this a written language or purely decorative? The symbols repeated down the pillar. She ran a finger over the rough surface, tracing the designs and leaving behind a smear of her blood. It was humanoid—two arms, two legs, and a torso.

Shadows shifted as the leaves moved, scattering the light. Caught on a raised ridge, a shadow cast over the symbol, giving the figure widespread wings, like an angel.

Or a demon.

Sarah stepped back. The light shifted again, and the figure transformed, wingless. She stepped to the right, and the wings returned.

Huh.

On inspection, the light and shadows cast the same illusion on all the pillars. Each figure was different, as if they told a story.

She slowly spun in place, watching the images play out on ancient stone pillars. The effect was overwhelming, making her chest ache from the effort of breathing, or perhaps that was the heat.

Desperately thirsty, she followed the sound of water. A thick layer of fallen leaves and dirt covered the floor. The shafts of sunlight provided just enough light for her to pick her way through the debris. After a few minutes, she found a fountain embedded in a wall.

A spout trickled out of a stone wall, splashing down into a small bowl. The overflowing water spilled into a larger pool at the bottom. Colored pieces of white, blue, and green tiles formed a geometric design. It was... pretty.

Sarah did not expect a fountain on an alien planet to be pretty or, honestly, as basic as it was. She expected something out of a movie with glowing blue lights and hovering. Everything hovered in space. Now that she was standing in front of a source of water on an alien planet, disappointed that it seemed like any other fountain you could buy at a garden center, Sarah realized the heat was playing tricks on her.

Water. Now.

She dipped her hand into the lower basin. The water was cool. She hesitated. There could be bacteria or some weird fungus waiting to make her life hell.

Ha. Joke's on the bacteria; my life is pretty miserable right now.

Dehydration was her immediate fate. Alien bacteria could get in line.

Sarah washed her hands, rinsing off the blood and doing her best to work out the dirt from the scrapes on her palms. Clean enough, she caught water in her cupped hands from the spout.

She sniffed the water. It smelled musty, but not foul. She was too thirsty to care.

The first swallow mostly spilled down her chin. The second she managed better, enjoying the cold water, but making a mess. She ignored good manners, drinking her fill.

Thirst satisfied, she did her best to rinse her face. Blood and dirt swirled in the water.

Rustling from above snagged her attention. Darkness clung to the ceiling between the shafts of light.

Something moved in the shadows above her.

Sarah fumbled for her phone, cursing as she turned on the flashlight function.

The phone's light barely pierced the shadows overhead. Yes, something was up there. She caught inky black figures shuffling in place. Feathers caught the light, shimmering blue on the edges. Feathers and eyes.

So many eyes.

The air felt suffocating. Blood pounded in her ears.

By the time Sarah realized she was looking at dozens, perhaps hundreds, of large black birds, a croaking call echoed in the chamber. She should run, or at least back away slowly. Or just run.

A growl echoed off the stone.

CHAPTER THREE

SARAH

THE BIRDS—HUNDREDS, definitely hundreds—cried out and moved. She threw up her arms to protect herself from the flurry of feathers and wings beating against the hot air.

Time to run.

Blindly, she dashed deeper into the complex. Almost immediately, she tripped over the uneven floor. Landing on her knees, she hissed in pain.

The low growl grew louder, and it lit up a primitive part of her brain that refused to stick around long enough to discover the source of the growling.

Nothing good, she knew.

A creature emerged from a shadowy pocket. Or maybe it was more accurate to say the light parted around the creature. Darkness swirled around it like a sinister miasma. Sarah's mind cataloged the animal's features—four legs, compact and muscular build like a big cat or a lean wolf, huge triangular ears, four eyes that reflected the light, and a shifting outline that pulsed with the pounding in her chest.

Teeth.

Lots and lots of teeth.

The creature lifted its head, sniffing the air. Blood had drawn the monster. Even now, she felt the sticky ooze of blood sliding down her face from her head wound. For a second, she felt like she was watching a nature documentary and the poor gazelle just realized they were toast.

The watering hole is an irresistible draw for prey and predator alike.

An entirely inappropriate giggle bubbled up from her gut because she was a gazelle, and she was definitely toast. Or whatever-that-was chow. Monster chow.

She rose to a crouch, her eyes never leaving the monster. The shadows pulsed around it. She felt around the ground for a rock, a handful of dirt, or anything to throw. The stones she encountered felt tiny, like pebbles.

Beggars couldn't be choosers.

She grabbed the stone and stood.

The monster growled, stepping forward.

She stepped back.

A second creature emerged from the shadows. Then a third. She was surrounded.

"You're a pack hunter," she said, like they would have a conversation rather than a short chase followed by screaming. "I hate nature documentaries, for the record. They suck, and you suck. All of you."

The monsters really weren't talkers. One sprang forward. She tossed her handful of pebbles and ran.

Something large and feathery swooped over her head. Shrieks echoed off the stone walls. The monsters yelped in pain.

Sarah paused long enough to realize a massive black bird fought one shadow creature. Talons lashed out, and wings beat fiercely. The creature snapped, teeth flashing. One moment, it seemed to have the bird captured in its jaws, then the shadows shifted, and the bird was airborne again.

A monster caught her from the side, slamming her back to the ground. She covered her face with her arms. Teeth clamped down on a leg. Pain remained at a distance, and dully she realized that her body was in shock.

Four malevolent eyes glared at her as the teeth sank into her flesh.

She kicked with her free leg, but she lacked the strength to do more than irritate the creature. It snarled; mouth full of her blood. This was it. Sarah realized certain truths about herself and the universe.

One: being yanked through a portal sucked.

Two: she was going to die, and she wasn't even wearing shoes.

Three: no one would know what happened to her.

Four: she wanted to live.

If, by some miracle, she survived this mauling, she'd make changes. No more hiding. No more punishing herself because of survivor's guilt. Robert wouldn't want that. She knew he'd want her to enjoy the life she had.

She'd spend time with people she liked and do things she enjoyed.

She was going to live, dammit.

Her hand raked along the ground, searching for something, anything, with which to fight back. All she found were dried -up leaves and loose soil. She tossed it at the monster, dirt raining down on her face.

The monster jerked away.

A being stood over her, a cool gray in the darkness. Black wings stretched out behind him, blocking the light. Alien, yes, but humanoid. Two arms. Two legs.

Male? The wide shoulders and trim build suggested male.

He stared blankly in front of her, then tilted his head, revealing a set of luminous blue eyes on the side of his head.

Four eyes.

He barked an order at her, but his words had no meaning.

Alien, remember.

Huffing in disgust, he pushed her to one side and crouched next to her in a shooting stance. He extended a wing, covering her. A silver pistol appeared in his hands. He picked off the monsters, sending them yelping.

The large bird swooped down, settling on his shoulder. He and the bird seemed to share a moment as he scratched its head and it cooed. Then it swiveled its head to watch her.

Four eyes. The bird had four eyes.

The wings evaporated like smoke, there one moment and gone the next. His skin turned as black as onyx. He stared down at her; all four eyes black.

She gulped, not sure if she should say something to break the tension or just go straight to the begging not to be murdered. "So—"

The black dissolved, again reminding her of swirls of smoke as it faded out of sight, leaving his cool gray complexion unmarked.

And that broke her. After being sucked into a portal, landing on an alien planet, falling through the roof, and whatever those monsters were, his trick with the wings was one thing too many for her brain to process.

Dizziness washed over her.

Now seemed like a good time to faint.

VEKELE

A pistol. How utterly pointless. He had grabbed it out of habit as he left the ship.

Useless.

Growling in frustration, Vekele kept the female pinned under a wing while he tried to hit the damnable void beast. They phased in and out of the shadows, never staying in one place for long. A hunter had to be extraordinarily skilled to hit one, let alone kill.

Let alone with only half his sight.

Ignoring the blurry area in the center of his field of vision, he concentrated on what he could do. He tilted his head to one side, anticipating where the beast would appear and firing a short burst. There was no need to hit the void beast; keeping it at bay would suffice. At least the female kept still under the shelter of his wing.

Eventually, Kenth and Luca arrived. Well-timed shots hit the beast and drove it away, proving the guards to be competent, if not timely. The skirmish over, he retracted his wings.

That was when the female fainted. Vekele caught her before she hit the ground.

She was... odd. Pinkish, but some of that could be the bloody wound on her head. Her hair was a flamboyant scarlet, dark brown at the roots. A chemical odor clung to the hair, and he could not understand why anyone would alter dark locks to such an unnatural color.

Everything about her seemed unnatural, down to her clothing.

And yet...

With his thumb and forefinger on her chin, he turned her head to the side.

Nothing, just a smooth expanse of skin. If she had been blinded or her eyes injured, perhaps removed due to disease, surely there would be scar tissue.

He ran a thumb over the unblemished skin. It was as if her second set of eyes had not existed at all. Odd. Odder still, he was intrigued rather than repulsed.

This female was not Arcosian. She was something else entirely.

"You call this staying back?" Kenth trotted up, fury in her tone. "Running into the unknown?"

"You were slow, Captain, and mind your tone." Vekele lifted his chin and pulled his shoulders back, still holding the strange female. He might be disfigured with two damaged eyes and no longer a soldier, but he was still a prince. Baris might find amusement in insubordination, but Vekele did not.

"You ignored a direct order, *Your Highness*," Kenth said, her tone cold and correct but full of dislike. Which suited Vekele. He required obedience, not approval.

"Again, you were slow." He turned his attention to the female.

The void beast savaged her leg. The wound bled profusely, soaking the fabric of her trousers. She required a medic, but he had enough practical experience to do the basics with a med kit.

He stripped off his tunic under the mantle. The female had lost a considerable amount of blood. No wonder she fainted. As he wrapped the fabric around the wound and applied pressure, he examined a design inked into the pink skin of her upper arm.

A karu.

Highly stylized but unmistakable, with the four eyes and wings spread wide.

Why did this stranger have the royal symbol etched into their flesh?

"Who is that?" Luca asked.

"Our anomaly," Vekele replied.

The two guards peered at the female in Vekele's arms. Despite their physiological differences—he shuddered at the horrible blankness on the side of her face—he felt drawn to her.

He checked behind her ear. No scarring to indicate an implanted translator. Curious.

"Is that a Nakkoni?" Luca asked.

"No. Nakkoni have scales and a tail," Kenth answered.

"Nakkoni shed their scales, don't they? And her tail could have been damaged. You never know with an alien."

"That is not a Nakkoni."

"Like you're an expert. They're colorful, and so is she," Luca said. After a pause, he added, "Some Khargals can shift their color."

"They have wings and stone skin. Does the female appear to have stone skin?"

Vekele's wings itched to burst forth and shield her from Kenth and Luca's eyes. Whoever she was, she was not a curiosity to be ogled.

"Enough," he barked. "She requires a medic."

"Is it female?" Luca asked, clearly not knowing when to be quiet.

Vekele rose to his feet. The flesh at his back and shoulders burned, then his wings went wide, knocking into the impertinent male. *Good.*

"Forgive me for not making the order explicitly clear. Return to the ship and prepare for departure, Luca." Vekele marched out of the temple, cradling the stranger to his chest. Her breathing remained steady, but he disliked how the pink color drained from her complexion.

His karu flew in front, scouting the way.

"Sir," the male said, his face blushing an unseemly shade of violet. He hurried after Vekele.

"Kenth, have a medical team ready to meet us when we land at the palace."

The older female nodded, then opened her mouth to speak. She hesitated.

"Out with it," Vekele ordered. These two were the best the royal guard had to offer? It was a miracle that his brother had not been assassinated.

"Your Highness," Kenth said in a cautious voice, "is that wise?"

Vekele blinked in the sunlight. Kenth had a point. This was a covert mission; to return to the castle with a medical team on standby would draw unwanted attention.

"You are correct," he said. Kenth's eyes went wide, surprised at Vekele's sudden shift to being reasonable. He continued, "We do not speak of the female. The anomaly was dust on a sensor."

Kenth and Luca nodded.

"Set a course for my residence. Send for my medic, Harol. Tell him I was stubborn and refused to wear the protective lenses on my eyes, and now I require a tonic for pain. Have him wait for our arrival," Vekele said.

Harol had been the field medic under his command. He trusted the male's discretion completely.

"Stubborn? You?"

Vekele turned to the female. *Jokes. Unbelievable.*

Kenth held his gaze. She did not appear shamed for unearned familiarity or the humor.

For a moment, Vekele felt a pang of yearning for the camaraderie of the military. The soldiers under his command had been obedient but did not spare his royal ego from teasing. In the year since Vekele's injury, no one had dared jest with him. Ignored him, tried to pretend that the youngest prince did not exist, pitied him, or lavished him with praise for *being brave* and preserving. Every interaction was tainted by acknowledgment of his damage, "polite" or otherwise.

Is it any wonder he hid himself away in an isolated house in the middle of nowhere?

At the palace, no one treated him as if he were a person.

Until this foolhardy guard.

Vekele understood why Baris thought so highly of the captain of the royal guard.

He sighed. "Harol would expect nothing less," he said.

Truthfully, a visit from Harol would not be amiss. A familiar ache grew behind his front eyes. The damage to his eyes meant the pupils failed to expand and contract correctly. He only noticed when he developed a headache. He should have worn the protective lenses, but he disliked the reminder of his injury and would rather endure the pain.

"Very good, sir."

Vekele marched up the ramp into the ship. They had an hour until they arrived at Summerhall. He would do what he could for the female and hoped it would be enough.

CHAPTER FOUR

SARAH

EVERYTHING HURT, so she wasn't dead.

The gray guy with the ears and all the eyes stood over her, frowning. In one hand, he held a bottle, and the other pointed to her leg.

Right. A nightmare puppy used her as a chew toy.

She hoped that was medicine and not poison, but her throat was too dry for snarky comments. Whatever. If it was poison, it was poison. There was nothing she could do about it.

She turned her head away as he cleaned the wound. It stung for a moment, then a numbness crept up her leg.

Dully, she realized she should be freaking out. Portal. Another world. Monsters. A girl was entitled to a freak -out, but a lifetime of stories had prepared her for magical portals leading to adventure. Alice had her rabbit holes. Wardrobes were notorious transportation devices, as were ruby slippers—or silver in the books.

Now Sarah had a cell phone-generated portal to an alien planet. Not a problem. The last few hours fit a familiar story shape, and that made it manageable.

They were in a sterile white room. She lay on top of a bed with pillows behind her back. The blanket felt scratchy.

A large window took up the majority of the opposite wall, framing twin moons.

Not Earth.

Yup, she should be freaking out.

Her eyes fluttered shut, too heavy to stay open. Maybe she'd have a proper freak -out after a nap.

SOMEONE MOVED her to an upright position and pressed a glass of water to her lips. They were not gentle as they tipped the water into her mouth.

Sarah coughed, dribbling water down her chin.

The gray guy frowned, which had to be his default expression.

The second attempt at drinking went better, with less dumping of an entire glass down her throat.

A hand roughly turned her face from side to side. More frowning. Muttering. A finger poked and prodded the side of the head.

Using all her energy, she leaned forward and reached for him with her good hand. Gently, she turned his face from side to side, imitating how he inspected her.

Caution flashed in the blue eyes on the side of his face. The ones in front remained dull and gray. She suspected the front ones were not the dominant eyes, which was a weird quirk of evolution, but whatever. She wasn't an alien expert or, you know, a biologist.

His ears were long and pointy, like an elf. His complexion was gray. Dark hair tumbled forward, shorter on the sides to not obscure his field of vision. His mouth pressed into a tight line, as if grumpy.

"I like your face," she said.

His mouth fell open.

It was cute, in a grouchy way.

VEKELE

The room was confining. Vekele paced from the bedroom, down the corridor, past his office, to the unused receiving room, and back again. He needed to move. He needed to stretch his wings. He had never been one to stand in place. Baris pointed him to a target, and Vekele did as his king commanded.

True, he had hidden away in these rooms in the last year. The attack had damaged more than his sight. An intangible spark had been doused.

Now… the female intrigued him. More than he cared to admit.

Returning to the country house undetected had been easy enough. The ship passed through the planetary security grid with ease, crossing zones with no questions asked. Traveling in the royal vessel had its privileges.

Once landed, there was a short but exposed distance to cross from the flyer to the house. The likelihood of being observed was small—Vekele was uninteresting and out of the political loop—but he chose to be cautious. He drew the shadows to him and wore the darkness like a cloak.

If anyone watched through a satellite feed, no one would question that the half-blind prince preferred to be unobserved. On most days, Vekele kept the shadows about him as a barrier. He did not enjoy being seen. Not like this. Not for some time.

Keeping out of the medic's way while he attended the female's injuries proved harder. Vekele brimmed with excess energy and curiosity. He wanted answers. Now. Perhaps he was as spoiled as Baris claimed but waiting tested his patience.

Princes should not have to wait, not even half-blind ones.

"The dramatics will not speed this along," Harol said, his eyes fixed on the female's torn flesh. The trousers had been removed and the flesh washed clean of debris.

Vekele's eyes slid past the exposed skin. Not that the curve of her calf was particularly attractive as Harol used a tool to knit the flesh together. Nor was it particularly gruesome. He had seen worse on the battlefield, but it felt wrong to watch; the female deserved a small amount of privacy.

After what felt like an eternity but was only minutes, Harol finished mending the leg and tended to the smaller injuries.

"The female spoke, but the ship's scanner could not locate the translator implant," Vekele said. The chip's manufacturer would give him a clue as to the female's origins.

Harol scanned the female, frowned at the results, and ran the scanner again. "No sign of an implanted translator chip."

"It is there."

"Are you certain you did not find a translator? Perhaps something decorative in her ear?"

"Nothing. The female wears no ornaments." Other than the design inked into her skin.

"Are you certain that she has a translator?"

"She spoke," Vekele repeated, tired of this conversation. No matter how the medic phrased the question, the female did not have a translator, yet she spoke flawless Arcosian.

"Perhaps it was only a string of chatter that sounded like Arcosian words," Harold suggested.

"No, she…" Vekele hesitated to finish the thought. "She said that she liked my face."

"Ah," the medic said, snapping shut the med kit. "It is not a bad-looking face. I daresay some find it handsome."

Vekele flushed, unsure why the medic's sarcastic flattery bothered him. The female had looked at him, considered his appearance, and seemed pleased. "She examined my features and spoke. It was not nonsense."

Harol's gaze settled on the female. After a moment, he nodded. "Perhaps Reilen or Nakkon have made advances in translator tech and my scanner is unable to detect it."

"I have considered that."

"I do not have the equipment here. Perhaps in the capital, but—"

"Her presence here must remain confidential," Vekele said, speaking over the medic. He trusted Harol. They served together on many campaigns. When the medic left the military, he returned to his home village, a small settlement nearby.

"Then I can think of one other possibility. She was infected by the void beast," Harol said.

"No." Impossible. The void beast carried the same parasite as the karu. While a karu formed a mutually beneficial relationship with a person, a void beast was a thoughtless creature. They did not bond. They tore their hosts apart. "Only a handful of people have ever survived bonding with a void beast, and that was centuries ago. They might as well be legends."

"How intriguing," Harol said, unmoved by the improbability of the notion.

Not how Vekele would phrase it, but to each his own.

"I dare say we will know for certain when the bonded beast shows up. I am done here," Harol continued. "I have a sample of her blood. I will test for infection and run a genetic analysis on her samples to discover her origin."

Vekele had put much thought into the female's origin. While the medic worked, he had nothing else to occupy his thoughts. He considered and eliminated all the planets and systems that used to be part of the

Arcosian trade network. In the end, he only had one possibility.

"I believe she is from Reilen," he said. It was not a good solution. Reilendeers considered themselves superior and regarded interaction with lesser lifeforms as a necessary evil to trade. They knew of the royal mark and would believe the Arcosians backward enough to revere a stranger bearing such a mark. As an infiltration tactic, it was efficient.

It made little sense, however. Trade between Arcos and Reilen had been halted for more than a century, thanks to war within the kingdom that left common merchant ships unprotected from pirates. Therefore, there was no reason for a Reilendeer to be present, let alone go through the trouble of inking the royal mark on an operative.

The medic's gaze swept over the female. "The coloring is correct, but Reilendeer have antlers."

Vekele had considered that as well. "They are shifters. Who knows what they are capable of? Why a Reilendeer would be in Arcosian territory remains to be seen."

"Well, it is above my pay grade to speculate," Harol said, his tone indifferent as he opened the med kit. He rattled off a list of instructions. "I have cleaned the wound, but she will require a bath. Keep her off the leg. Rest. Expect a fever. This is for pain as needed. No more than two."

A pill bottle rattled as Harol set it on a side table.

"Is it safe?" Vekele asked. They did not know the female's biology or if she could tolerate the same drugs as an Arcosian. "I did not retrieve this female from Miria only to have her accidentally poisoned."

Harol tilted his head. "Is that the only reason? Bad manners?"

"Doubtless my brother could turn an elegant phrase about hospitality and the inexcusable rudeness of murdering a guest, but I am a simple male."

The medic huffed with amusement. "The female has tolerated the sedative thus far. If her mind is clear, let her be aware of the risks and decide."

"When she wakes, we will have much to discuss."

He stood at the foot of the bed, finally looking at the female. She seemed small in his bed, swallowed up by the pillows and layers of blankets, and not attractive. Red hair clung to her scalp. Feverish, her skin was drained of color and too pink all at once.

Harold had removed her garments for access to her wounds, but she carried the dust and debris from the temples of Miria. Blood still clung to her skin. She was a filthy, sweaty lump, ruining his fine sheets.

Oddly, even ill, and unattractive in her current condition, she appeared correct, as if his bed had been a lonely place waiting for this female with red hair.

A bath.

The medic prescribed a bath.

He swallowed, picturing the female soaking in a bath. Fragrant blossoms would be scattered across the water. Sweet soaps, aromatic oils, and the richest lotions would line the tub, ready for her selection.

The karu hopped from the headboard to the foot of the bed, squawking to interrupt his inappropriate thoughts. The female was injured. She was unwell.

It would be proper to summon an attendant to bathe her, but her presence needed to remain hidden for the moment. He could do an adequate job with a basin of water and a cloth.

"You have your instructions, Your Highness." Harol packed up his supplies to leave.

"Leave the kit," Vekele said.

The medic stiffened. "Sir, if you intend to use my tools of healing to inflict harm—"

"No," he interrupted, surprised.

"During your *discussion*." Harol squared his shoulders, preparing himself to be struck for his insolent tone.

Vekele sighed. He could not blame the male. In recent years, the military had a reputation for employing unsavory means to acquire information. His own

family had been known to torture secrets out of each other.

Not to mention the long tradition of abduction and murder.

That the medic expected Vekele to torture his female—his *guest*—was all the motivation he needed to keep Baris on the throne. Arcos desperately needed a leader who could imagine a world at peace. Plenty of blood-thirsty warriors had worn the crown, and the kingdom had suffered.

Arcos needed Baris, and Vekele would do anything to secure Baris' reign.

In a cool voice, he said, "If I require additional supplies, it is better to have a bandage on hand than to summon you and draw attention. I will not undo your good work by injuring the…" He hesitated to use the word prisoner. "Our guest."

"Our guest," Harol repeated, testing out the concept. He nodded, satisfied. Then he tilted his head, regarding Vekele. "And how is your headache?"

"Tolerable," he admitted.

The ache from damaged tissue and overly sensitive nerve endings was a constant companion. Occasionally, he glimpsed color or movement in his forward vision range, but it was nothing. Only shadow. The phenomenon reminded him of the older soldiers who lost a limb and reported that they could still feel the ache.

He barely noticed.

"You are done," he said, dismissing the medic.

Now alone, he considered his next steps. Torture and punishment did not yield quality results. Only a fool relied on pain to gather intelligence. Bargaining was effective. Greed motivated many.

He considered all that he had to offer the female. He was a prince, after all. The Arcosian kingdom spanned planets. Its grandeur may have faded in the last century, but it contained many treasures.

Her red hair against the white linen was like a slash of scarlet blood on fresh snow.

Such an ostentatious color. Did she never know the need to hide in the shadows? Was the world she came from safe enough to make herself an obvious target?

His mission was clear now. He filled a basin with warm water and soap. The female required bathing. He could perform this task.

The mattress dipped as he sat beside the female. Starting with her face, he gently worked the damp sponge over her. Carefully, he skirted around the blank spot on the side of her head where her eyes should be. The worst of the grime had dried and matted in her hair. He would need more than a sponge to clean that.

With clinical detachment, he worked his way along her shoulders and down her arms. He wiped away the dirt to examine the design inked on her skin.

It was unmistakably the royal mark, a karu with outstretched wings, framed by a moon. The black ink was not fresh, but not entirely faded.

Curious.

When she woke, he would interrogate—no, question—her and conduct a risk assessment. He would smother her with tenderness and care until she spilled all her secrets.

Having a mission, even one he designed for himself, eased the tension in his chest. It felt familiar, and he welcomed the task.

CHAPTER FIVE

SARAH

THE THIRD TIME SARAH WOKE, she was chained to a bed.

Naked.

Because that was a thing that happened to her now.

In all fairness, it was a very nice bed. The best she'd ever had the pleasure of being chained to. The sheets felt like water against her skin, soft and flowing. The mattress might as well have been a giant marshmallow; it was extra cushy, along with the pillows.

The gray elf sat beyond the foot of the bed in an overly elaborate high-backed black chair, complete with ornate scrollwork. A large black bird perched on the back of the chair. Leaning to one side, the man casually lounged with a hand resting on his knee as he watched her. He looked bored. He might as well have a sign flashing "Villain!" directly over his head.

No, that wasn't fair. He saved her from the shadow monsters.

"Hey, hey," she said, her voice little more than a croak. "Hey!"

The bird squawked, and the man leaned forward, no longer pretending to be bored.

"Water? And maybe some clothes."

With a sigh, he pushed himself out of the chair toward a side table and poured water from a pitcher with a surprising amount of attitude from a man who hadn't spoken a word to her.

He set it down on the bedside table, tossed a navy-blue robe onto the bed, then left without a word. The bird stayed behind, watching.

Creepy, but sure. Roll with it.

"I don't suppose you talk," she said, her voice dry and rasping.

No response, but the bird's eyes had an intelligent gleam—all four of them—like it was taking the measure of her worth.

Wow. Dramatic much? Sarah apparently fell through a portal into a melodrama.

At least her sense of sarcasm still worked.

She pushed herself into an upright position. Her back ached. Her shoulders burned. Her head spun. Everything hurt, like she fell through a ceiling and then into the jaws of a shadowy beast with way too many teeth.

Sitting at the edge of the bed, she stretched and flexed her feet. Her leg was... okay. A film wrapped around her calf, transparent and glossy. Through the film, her skin appeared red, but not nearly as bad as Sarah would have expected, considering the monster had its jaws solidly around her leg.

Moving stiffly, she bent over and poked the damaged area.

Sarah hissed. Okay, not her brightest idea. While still tender to the touch, the area looked mostly healed. Bruising on her calf was a mottled green, definitely not what it should look like the day after.

More like two weeks after.

She needed a mirror, but didn't see one immediately. She twisted in place to get a better look at herself, muscles burning in protest. Angry green bruising blossomed across her hip.

Strange. It should have been purple and blue at this stage. How long had she been asleep?

She slipped on the robe and gulped down the water. The robe felt divine, soft, and silky. Gold embroidery decorated the collar and cuffs.

Minutes ticked by. The bird tucked its head down, resting.

The room was very nice in that way that shouted that it was very expensive, but it was also faded and dusty. Once, this room had been the epitome of grandeur, splashing money and tons of it, but the glory days were behind it.

She noticed the silence, the absolute stillness in the room. There were no noises from outside the window, no clatter of traffic, or murmured voices from the hall. This place felt isolated, possibly forgotten.

The layer of dust certainly added to the forgotten vibe. A place this huge—assuming all the rooms were this size—needed a large staff for maintenance.

Unless Mr. Grumpy did all the housework himself.

Sarah looked around the room and got in the impression that he did not.

She took in the ornate wood panels, the gilded everything, crystal for the sake of crystal, and the mural on the ceiling. Silken draperies hung from floor to ceiling, blocking the natural light, but the genuine crystal chandelier provided enough light. If she had been in a futuristic room before, now she had somehow fallen back to Marie Antoinette's Versailles, only dustier.

Electric lights glowed in the crystal above. A soft whirring noise of moving air betrayed a ventilation system.

So not the eighteenth century. Wherever she was, they just happened to share the aesthetic of executed monarchs.

Sarah tested the chain. Despite being as thin as a delicate necklace, it proved durable. Her stomach growled and her bladder ached.

Yeah, that was a thing that she couldn't ignore. Looking around the room, she spotted a door sitting ajar. That might not have been a bathroom, but she needed to check it out.

She pushed herself to her feet, dismayed to find her legs had been replaced with noodles. Clutching the bed frame for support, she hobbled to a nearby chair. The chain expanded, allowing her to move. Navigating her way along the room via furniture, she made her way to the mystery door.

It was a simple bathroom with the necessary plumbing. With that done, she washed up and hobbled back out into the bedroom.

The chain stretched as far as the window. She pulled back moldering drapes, dust heavy in the air. Years of grime clouded the windows, creating a layer of fog-like distortion over the landscape.

It was gorgeous and terrifying.

An endless forest sprawled out in every direction. The house was perched high enough to offer unobstructed views of the rolling hills. A mist settled in the valley.

The trees were the deep, verdant green of summer. They appeared familiar yet wrong at the same time.

Immediately surrounding the house was an overgrown, abandoned garden. Thick hedges gave the impression that the garden had once been carefully maintained.

Like a fairytale.

It remained to be seen if this was an "eaten by the Big Bad Wolf" fairy tale or a "sweet, happily ever after with a prince" fairytale.

Considering that she woke up naked and chained to a bed, she didn't like her odds of a happy ending. No, that wasn't entirely true. Her mysterious benefactor rescued her and gave her medical care. So, fifty-fifty?

Robert would love this.

She tensed. The thought came unbidden. She expected it to hurt, but it didn't. Her heart ached, like the way her bad knee did after she fell on an icy sidewalk two years ago. Not terrible, but enough to know that pain would always be her companion.

Tolerable.

Her grief was tolerable. Well, that was something. If she ever got back home and had another appointment with her counselor, they'd call it progress.

Another goal in the action plan.

All at once, she was furious with Robert for leaving her without a chance to say goodbye. How dare he leave her? He was her best friend, and now she was smack dab in the middle of an awesome adventure, and she couldn't share it with him. It was unfair and made her chest hurt.

Her hands clutched the aging draperies, the fabric crushed in her grip. Tears welled up, blurring her vision. She couldn't stop crying if she tried. It felt like too much for one person to contain. She fell through a portal, landed on an alien planet, got mauled by a shadow monster, got rescued, and woke up chained—albeit with a tasteful chain—to a bed in a moldering fairy tale palace. Just... what was she supposed to do with all this?

"Okay, okay," she whispered to herself. Her breath hitched between words. She had a lifetime of stories to guide her on what to do next. People searched for a way home. Dorothy did it. Hell, even Odysseus did it, eventually.

New action plan...

Her mind went blank. She needed more information, which was as good of an action plan as anything. Make an ally, which meant first contact, and that was a whole thing, because *aliens*. Get questions answered. Where was she? What the hell happened? How could she get home? Whether or not she wanted to return home to her empty apartment and frustrating bookstore job,

Sarah wasn't going to think too deeply about it. Try to enjoy the adventure.

That felt... all right. The guilt she expected didn't surface. Robert would love every second of this, and while it sucked he wasn't there, this was a thing she could do to honor him. And that was almost like a thing they could share.

She spent the last three years hiding from her grief, friends, family, and the world. No more.

Dammit, more tears.

Sarah swiped at her eyes, irritated at how fragile she felt. Physically, she was okay-ish. Yes, naked and chained to a bed. That could have been better. Minus one point. But—and this was a big but—she was not dead. Someone, probably Mr. Sexy Dark Elf, gave her medical care and cleaned her up. Her body hurt, but more like she'd fallen through a portal than someone had drugged her drink. No one took advantage of her body while she was unconscious. One point.

Adventure! It's sort of meh on the whole.

Even in her mind, the wry tone was too dry to tolerate.

She was too caught up in her pity party to notice a door opening or her rescuer-captor entering the room.

"If you are planning an escape, you will fail," he said.

VEKELE

The female jumped at his words. She clutched at her chest. "Oh!"

She had no right to be so striking, standing at the window in his silk robe, bathed in the afternoon sunlight. It irritated him.

He crossed the room to the table near the windows and set the tray down with unnecessary force. The plate and cutlery rattled.

"What is wrong with your chest?" he asked. "Is your respiration at sufficient levels? How is your cardiac health?"

She blinked at him. One eye. Then the other.

He shivered at the wrongness of the sight.

"You startled me. I'm fine." Her stomach growled. She placed a hand over her abdomen, failing to stifle the sound. "Well, hungry. Is that food?"

She eyed the nutritional bars. He understood her doubt. The field rations provided enough fuel to maintain a body, but consuming the meals was an ordeal. He pointed to the chair in an unspoken command to sit. "Eat. We have much to discuss when you are finished."

"Are you sure that's food?" Despite her skepticism, she sat at the table and pulled a plate toward her. The bars jiggled with the motion. "Space jello."

Her words were nonsensical.

"It is the cook's day off," he said. Unbelievably, she flashed her blunt teeth at him and laughed.

Laughed.

"You threaten me? I am no chef, but it is not that bad," he said.

Vekele took the opposite chair. Well, perhaps it was believable. Field rations were an offense against anyone with functioning taste buds.

She pressed her lips together, then pushed the plate away. "Look, it's not that I'm ungrateful. Thank you for saving me and patching me up, by the way. A-plus quality hero work. But I'm not entirely convinced this isn't your murder shack in the mountains and I'm going to be a head you mount on a wall."

He understood all her words individually, but together they made an incomprehensible mess.

"If I wanted you dead, I would have left you at Miria as a sacrifice to the old spirits there," he said.

"Yeah, that's what I think, but," she waved a hand broadly to the room, "murder shack. It's nice. A very nice murder shack. Very pre-French Revolution."

More nonsense words, yet he understood her meaning. As a gesture of peace and goodwill, he unsheathed the blade strapped to his lower leg and placed it on the table. "I do not attack from behind, and if I did, I would use this."

Her eyes went wide at the sight of the knife. He understood why; it was a very impressive knife.

"That's not as reassuring as you think it is, but you can do this." She slid the plate toward him and tapped the table, waiting.

The presumption of this female. Behind him, the karu watched from her perch on the headboard. He felt her amusement through the bond.

"I am Prince Vekele of the House Shadowmark. You are my guest," he said.

"Sarah Krasinski," she replied. She stared at him, waiting.

He plucked the bar off the plate and took a bite. "I do not poison guests. It is horribly ill-mannered."

This appeased her. She picked up a piece, brought it to her mouth, and then paused. "If I eat this, am I forever bound to your realm? Or are you trying to trick me into being your servant for a hundred years?"

"No," he said, his voice flat.

"Just had to check." She popped the morsel into her mouth. Her eyes went wide as she struggled to chew, then swallow. She coughed. "Wow, how is it chewy and slimy at the same time?"

"It is nutritionally balanced, not appetizing." An unpleasant truth many soldiers learned. She reached for the cup, sniffing the contents. He understood her cautiousness. "It is a slurry of fruit, fruit juice, vegetable matter, and protein powder. Your body requires additional fuel while you recover from your injuries."

"Mmm, a slurry." Her tone mocked, but she closed her eyes and drank. They shot back open in surprise. "It's a chocolate and banana smoothie. Why did you let me eat the slimy jello cubes when there's a chocolate banana smoothie?"

"Because I poisoned the beverage," he answered.

She blinked. It was so disturbing. Then she laughed.

His shoulders tensed, bristling at the insult of being laughed at. Slowly, he realized the female found his comment amusing.

"Explain the mark on your arm," he said, no longer able to resist asking. Yes, he was too eager to know. A skilled agent would pick up on this and use it against him.

"This?" Sarah rubbed the royal mark. "It's an owl. I thought it was funky."

"Funky." Such a ridiculous word.

"Curious?" She refilled the cup with water and drank, watching him over the brim.

He did not have the patience to play her games. "Does this owl have significance on your Earth?"

"Sure. There's lots of folklore about owls. Generally, they're symbols of wisdom."

"Do they have the correct number of eyes?"

"What?" Her brow furrowed in confusion. "Just two. Like I said, my tattoo is funky."

Interesting. Vekele was intrigued by her decision to modify the design but kept his thoughts to himself.

"Why do you want to know?" she asked.

"It is a funky design," he replied in a dry tone.

She rolled her eyes. "Fine, be all mysterious."

He watched the female as she finished her meal, trying to determine if she was a spy. Other than the quips, she said nothing of substance.

A useful skill for a spy to possess.

However, her face betrayed her thoughts. She spoke before thinking. Vekele could not believe this female was anyone's first choice as an operative.

He already knew she was a human from Earth, wherever that was. The genetic sample Harol took indicated a little-known primitive species on the fringe of the galaxy. Records were out of date, but the most recent information indicated that humans were nowhere near achieving interstellar flight.

How did this pretty human arrive on Arcos?

Perhaps she was on Arcos to cause chaos.

Vekele watched as she chased a bite-sized morsel around the plate with a fork. Finally, she picked it up with her fingers, then stabbed it with the utensil. She grinned in triumph.

Yes, chaos seemed to be in her skill set.

Her arrival days before the royal engagement and peace treaty could not be a coincidence.

Citizens of Reilen and Duras had traveled to Earth—wherever that was—yet they had no motive to disrupt Baris' fragile peace.

The noble families who opposed Baris had every motive, but not the means. Vekele doubted that a single vessel in the royal fleet could make a significant journey out of the system. Maintaining trade within the kingdom and the far territories alone strained the resources of the aging Arcosian fleet.

The karu fluffed her feathers and clicked her beak. He sensed her frustration through their bond.

It did not matter how the female arrived on his planet. The only question was, what was he going to do with her?

SARAH

Sarah didn't understand herself. This was *first contact*. This was serious, yet here she was, sharing a meal with an elven prince—albeit a cranky one—and she kept cracking jokes. She needed to charm him and convince him to help her. Not... whatever this train wreck was.

She felt fragile, tension and anxiety winding tighter and tighter inside until she'd either explode into sobs or laughter. So smartass comments it was, for her mental wellbeing and keeping her shit together.

Prince Vekele made it easy. He had a face...okay, look; he was gorgeous. Weird, but gorgeous. All elves were. That was their thing. Dark hair hung forward. His lips pressed together cruelly—again, elf. Cruel seemed to be the default, according to certain fairy tales.

He thought he was so intimidating, and honestly? He was. His front eyes were a cloudy gray and reacted slowly to the light, giving him an air of intensity.

Someone cleaned her and tended her wounds. Someone put her in a soft bed with clean sheets, the cleanest thing in a dusty, disused house. Someone made her drink water when she drifted in and out of consciousness. She hadn't been unconscious the entire time she was ill. She heard the concern in his voice when he spoke to the doctor. His words had been firm, even harsh, but his touch had only ever been gentle.

Prince Vekele could pretend to be a scary badass all he wanted. She knew.

"So," she said, setting down the empty cup, "what are we talking about?"

"You will tell me who you are, how you came to Arcos, and your objectives," he blurted, as if he had a list ready to go. He probably did. "Do not lie or lie by omission. I will know."

"I believe you," she said, meaning every word. Nerves fluttered in her gut; unsure what Prince Vekele would do if he thought she held back. She was already chained to his bed. The next logical step would be the dungeon.

"I've told you my name: Sarah Krasinski. I'm from Philadelphia, on the planet Earth. I work in a bookstore, but you don't really want to know that. Okay, okay. I'm not sure how I got here. My phone did a... thing. A portal or wormhole. Look, I can't describe it better than that. I work in a freaking bookstore, not NASA. I got sucked through the portal and you know the rest."

He tilted his head, considering her while she babbled. When she finished, he did not speak immediately.

She picked up the empty smoothie cup. The food had been filling, but she craved more. "Can I have another? I don't know why I'm so hungry."

"Your body is fighting an infection and using more energy than normal," he said.

"An infection?" She glanced down at her leg. The injury appeared to be healing well.

"The parasite from the bite. Do not be concerned—"

"Parasite!" Sarah jumped up from the table, waving her hands like she could shake off the parasite. Her skin crawled with the sudden need for a scalding hot shower, lots of soap, and a vat of industrial-strength bleach. "What is it? Is it a tapeworm? It's a tapeworm. I've got an alien tapeworm. How do I get it out?"

"Remain calm. It is unlikely to bond with a human."

"Easy for you to say. You don't have a parasite living in you."

The bird laughed.

Hand to her heart, the bird tossed back its head and gave a short burst of caws that might as well have been laughing.

"Incorrect. Mine allows me to have a symbiotic relationship with the karu. We are bonded," he said.

That didn't sound terrible.

"Will I be bonded?"

"No. You were infected by a bite from a void beast."

"Right, right. The murder puppies."

He stared at her, his front eyes cloudy and unblinking.

This wasn't weird. At all.

"Am I a prisoner?" she asked.

He took too long to answer. Eventually, he said, "You are a guest of the crown."

Basically a prisoner. "Can we discuss the chain?"

"No."

"You chained me to your bed," she said.

"It is a very long chain."

"It's still a chain." She ran a hand through her hair and sighed. "I'll behave. Where would I even go? Unless there's a spaceship right outside that door, I'm stuck. I don't know where I am, I have no money, and no resources. Fuck, I don't even have underwear." As soon as she said the words, she wanted to claw them back.

Vekele tilted his head, watching her.

Great, now he was thinking about her lack of underwear.

"Metaphorically speaking," she added, a bit too late to be convincing.

"It is not a metaphor. You are wearing my robe and nothing else. I know. I undressed you and bathed you."

Well, when he said it like that, it was unsexy and borderline creepy.

Time to redirect the conversation.

"How can I get rid of the chain?" Sarah lifted her foot and gave it a shake.

"When I have decided you are not a threat or useful," he answered.

"I'm not a threat."

"You are a disruption, at the very least." His tone made her sound like the most dangerous woman in existence.

She needed to convince him she was as harmless as a bookstore clerk who had no social life and barely kept herself fed, because that's exactly what she was.

"Well, thanks for the rescue and patching me up," she said.

He scowled. Honest to goodness, hand over heart, he scowled like she hid a secret code in her words.

"Return to the bed," he ordered, his tone brooking no questions. "You have not recovered. I will not have you undo the medic's work."

"Right. I wouldn't want to be rude."

He gathered up the dishes and left, scowling, with some glowering added in for variety.

Sarah flopped back onto the bed. First contact was a bust. In retrospect, she should have doled out bits of information to Vekele in exchange for having her questions answered. As it was, she skipped over her entire life story and he told her the bare minimum: his name, his title, that she had a parasite that probably wouldn't kill her, and the name of the planet.

Oh, and he wouldn't poison a guest because he had manners.

Good job, Sarah. Minus one adventure point.

Minutes ticked by, but the corridor outside the room remained silent. Vekele wasn't coming back with another smoothie.

She did learn one thing he tried to keep from her.

The prince was blind.

CHAPTER SIX

SARAH

A DAY PASSED. Then another. Sarah found it hard to keep track of the days. Sometimes nightmares tore her from her sleep, vicious dreams about losing her family and running. So much running.

She woke, panting and in a cold sweat. The dreams were so real.

"You are safe." Vekele sat at the foot of the bed. Moonlight picked silver highlights in his dark hair. His gray complexion had an ethereal glow. It was unfair how pretty he looked when Sarah had a serious case of bedhead going on.

"Drink this," he said, pressing a glass into her hands.

It was warm and smelled medicinal, like spearmint or ginger, with a generous dose of disinfectant. She took a cautious sip, finding the beverage bitter. "Is it poison?"

He frowned. "No. We discussed this."

"Yeah, yeah. It's impolite to poison your hostages."

"Captive is more accurate. Hostage implies you will be traded for someone or something of equal value."

Sarah sipped the bitter drink, waiting for the punchline.

A bag of dirt. A bucket of rocks.

The punchline never came. He said, "It is tea to help you sleep. Drink."

His commanding tone was not to be ignored, and she was too tired to argue, so she downed the tea.

The tea acted quickly. She buried her face in her pillow, dismayed to find it soaked from drool but too sleepy to do anything about it.

When she woke, she had a burst of energy, but that soon faded, and she returned to bed. Her hunger never felt satisfied, no matter how generous the portions Vekele served. She felt hot and clammy. The air did not move, and Vekele only allowed the windows to open a crack.

Clothing arrived. Neatly folded, the fabric had a decadent feel and a light weight suitable for the warm days. The trousers were too long, and the blouse fit too snugly over her chest. The waistcoat had an outrageously stiff and elaborate collar that made her feel as if she were about to lure children into a gingerbread house for a snack. Considering the air of abandonment in the palace, Sarah wondered if the clothes were antique.

She spoke to no one except Vekele and the bird. When Vekele left to do whatever it was he did—polish his daggers, practice his sneer—the bird remained. The more time Sarah spent with the bird, the more she was convinced it wasn't an ordinary bird. Well, alien bird.

It watched her, intelligence shining behind all four eyes.

Overall, her captivity was unnerving and boring. So, so boring.

Vekele carried in another tray.

"More slurry?" she asked, sitting at the table.

"You have not objected to the beverage."

"I'm objecting to the name."

"And *smoothie* is better? It is not smooth. The fruit has been pulverized into a fine texture," he said.

"Which is smooth."

"Which is a slurry."

Sarah pressed her lips together to fight her smile. If he thought she enjoyed this, he'd stop talking to her. So far, Vekele carefully avoided disclosing any real information. Where was she? His house. What planet? His planet.

That was fine. She'd talk in circles with him, as long as she got to talk to another living person. Chattering at the giant bird was good, but that only got her so far. A die-hard introvert, Sarah was fine on her own.

That's not true, she mentally corrected herself. In the last few years, pain made her retreat and hide like a wounded animal. She liked people, generally. Robert had been the quiet one, perfectly content to let Sarah drag him to backyard cookouts and hang with their friends.

This situation was different. She couldn't hide and hope for the best. Too much was unknown here, and it weighed on her. She needed more than sitting alone in a decrepit palace bedroom with only a giant bird for company.

"Entertain me," she said.

"I am a prince. I am not here to entertain you."

"What about a game? Chess? Poker? Mario?" She mimed holding a game controller and wiggled imaginary toggles with her thumbs.

His foggy gray eyes blinked slowly, then his head tilted. "I do not play games."

"I'm bored," she said.

"That is not my concern."

"You said you wouldn't torture me."

"I have not. I provide food, water, garments, and shelter." His tone sounded genuinely offended.

"And socialization? Humans are social creatures," she said. It was a long shot, but worth a try.

"Most sapient beings are social. That is a hallmark of civilization," he retorted.

Fail.

"I need mental stimulation. I'm bored, and if I'm bored, I'm going to try to escape," she said, changing tactics. Appealing to his compassion hadn't worked, so now it was time for threats. The chain seemed indestructible, and the bed was too heavy to break without an ax. How she would escape, she didn't know, but that was Future Sarah's problem.

"You assured me you would not attempt to escape," he said. For the first time, his mask slipped, and he seemed concerned. "You are in an unknown location and have no resources."

"Oh, it'd be against my best interests, absolutely, but humans aren't always rational. In fact, we can be rather spiteful."

"You would escape only to wander through the forest and die of exposure or dehydration… out of spite?"

Sarah did her best to maintain a carefree expression. She wasn't an outdoorsy person and had zero wilderness survival skills. An alien bear would eat her so fast. "Yup. Spite."

Vekele made a disgruntled noise.

"Look, I know you don't want to talk because you're worried I'll wheedle state secrets out of you. Fine. Can we watch a movie or read a book? Teach me a game?"

He stood abruptly, jostling the table. For a moment, Sarah feared she'd gone too far. "Very well, if it will keep you from damaging yourself. Remain there."

Before long, he returned carrying a round board.

"Karu and Beasts," he said, laying out the pieces. Black and white pegs were separated into two piles. An animal head decorated the top of the peg. Some were teardrop-shaped, suggesting a bird's profile, and the others had pointy, triangular ears. Each piece was intricately carved with two eyes in the front and two on the side.

Sarah held a piece up to the light to examine it.

"Do not drop the karu. The set is very old," Vekele said.

"Is that what the bird is? A kah-rue?" She gestured to the ever-present bird with the peg.

"She is not a bird. She is a karu, a sacred being. And I am playing the karu." He plucked the token out of her hand, replacing it with the one with pointy ears.

Interesting. Before she could ask a question, he launched into explaining the rules.

"Listen carefully. I will not repeat myself. These are your warriors." He held up the peg with the pointy ears, the beast, to demonstrate. "Move your warriors through the labyrinth, toward the center. We roll dice to move. Capture your opponent's forces. The game is over when someone reaches the center. The one with the most warriors on the board is victorious."

"And the symbols on the board and dice? Do they mean something?" The symbols meant nothing to her. She turned the dice until the side with one dot showed. "One?"

"Obviously."

"But the board? Those aren't numbers." Symbols had been painted onto the wooden board and worn away in places.

"Those are special maneuvers. I will tell you what they say when it is necessary."

"If you're not cheating."

He drew back, shoulders square. "I do not cheat."

The pure scandal in his voice delighted her.

This was fun.

The first round went fast, with Vekele capturing nearly all her beasts. He didn't gloat, but his lips twitched, a momentary lapse in his haughty exterior that suggested he—gasp—enjoyed himself.

Or enjoyed trouncing Sarah.

By the third round, she had a better grasp on how the game flowed. While a large percentage was random and couldn't be controlled, knowing when to capture your opponent's pieces and when to let them pass could win the game.

Vekele leaned forward, head tilted and peering at the board. For someone who didn't play games, he was invested.

Then, without prompting, he crossed the room to open a window. Humid evening air flooded in, carrying the scent of flowers and grass.

The bird flew in, wide black wings beating loudly in the room. Sarah felt it brush by as it passed overhead before perching on the back of Vekele's chair.

"What's the bird's name?" she asked.

"The karu does not have a name." He resumed his seat, his posture upright, stiff, and reserved.

"Everything has a name."

He rolled the dice and gave a weary sigh.

Oh, her prince was all dramatic.

"She is ancient among her kind. Being chosen for a bond is an immense honor. I do not presume to name such a being," he said.

Sarah made an agreeable noise, nodding her head. "But what does she think about it? Can you tell through the bond?"

The karu in question perched on the back of Vekele's chair. A small rodent hung limply from her beak. She shook her head and swallowed it whole.

Sarah could never unsee that.

"She thinks you are too squeamish," he said, his voice warm and—unbelievably—amused.

"Don't laugh at me. That was…"

"Perfectly natural."

"Something, okay." Something she never wanted to see again, but the karu probably thought the way she ate was unnerving, too. "Did she really say that?"

He stroked the karu's head, gently gliding his fingers over smooth black feathers. "The bond is imprecise. I have impressions of her thoughts and emotions, but not exact words. To answer your previous question, I am an egg. Her egg. I cannot name her, but she is… agreeable to the concept of a name."

It took Sarah a second to sift through his words to find his meaning. Vekele was her baby, and the baby didn't name the parent.

It was adorable.

"She wants me to name her?" Sarah asked.

"She would not object—"

Sarah gasped in delight.

"But she is an ancient—"

"Yeah, yeah," Sarah said, speaking over him. "Ancient, honorable, and dignified."

The karu studied her with enough intensity to make Sarah squirm. The karu was regal in a way that made Sarah feel as if she tarnished the room with her presence, like she classed down the place.

Definitely not a Muffins or Birdy McBeakface name situation. The karu needed a serious name.

"I'll think on it," she said.

Vekele gave a grunt that sounded vaguely like approval.

The next round went swiftly, with Vekele claiming all her pieces in less than three moves.

"How long—" she started, but he spoke over her.

"No. I answered your question. Now you answer mine."

"Sure. That's fair," she said. Anything to keep him talking. She learned more about Vekele and the karu in the last few minutes than she had in days.

"Do you have a mate?" He moved his piece along the board. Everything in his body language said he couldn't be bothered about her answer, but his eyes watched her carefully.

"Mate like friend or mate like spouse?"

"Do not be evasive."

"Hey, I'm asking for clarification. I wasn't married, but I was engaged. He died." She paused, expecting pain to make her voice quiver, but the pain never came.

Vekele watched her, not bothering to hide the way his gaze swept over her. He seemed... hungry. He did not offer any platitudes or condolences, which she appreciated.

Sarah had grown so numb to people being sorry for her loss that resentment flared in her chest when she heard the words. Her *loss*, like a whole damn person could be boiled down to something so trivial. Robert hadn't been a lost trinket, and she wasn't a little sad. Her fucking heart had been cut out, and now she was some undead creature wandering through a half-life without a heart.

She blinked back tears.

Dammit.

"You are upset," Vekele said.

"The prince of observation," she muttered.

"I will leave." He gathered up the game pieces.

"No. Stay," she said hurriedly. She couldn't bear to sit alone in the room again. "Stay, please. I'm not upset."

"You are weeping."

Sarah wiped her eyes with the cuff of the blouse. Instinct wanted to say it was complicated and ignore the subject, but she had a feeling that Vekele wouldn't let the subject go so easily.

Gotta face it head -on.

"We've got a saying that time heals all wounds," she said. "But no one mentions that you're not the same. You've got scar tissue, and mostly you forget about it, but sometimes it hurts."

He nodded. "That is an astute observation."

Now that she was talking about Robert, actually talking and not pretending that everything was fine, she couldn't stop. "He died in his sleep. A brain aneurysm. The doctors said there was a weak area in a blood vessel, and it was bound to happen. Nothing anyone could do about it."

"Human brains do that? That is a defective design."

"It's not a defect. Robert wasn't defective," she snapped.

His brows rose in surprise.

Needing a few moments to collect herself, she sipped her glass of water. Once drained, the glass thumped on the table. She said, "He made me laugh. He was caring and kind. He was my friend, and I love him. Loved him."

Vekele refilled the glass. "Now you are angry with me and no longer weeping. Good," he said in a pleased tone.

That smug bastard.

"How about you? Do you have a mate?" Let's see how he liked it when the tables were turned.

"No. I am a prince. My mate will be whoever the king selects."

That seemed cold. "What if you don't love them?" she asked.

"My feelings in the matter are irrelevant. I must think of the crown. My duty is clear," he said.

Despite the firmness in his tone, she heard a longing in his voice that called to her.

VEKELE

Vekele was not a cook. Why would he be? There was always someone in the palace to prepare meals. In the military, self-serve appliances delivered meals on demand. When those broke—and they always did—he gnawed on a ration bar. At Summerhall, someone from the village came once a week to deliver supplies, mostly bland rations. Vekele never made requests and had been content to survive on what he had been given.

The meals he had prepared for Sarah seemed inadequate now, despite being nutritionally sound. Even though she disliked the ration bar, she consumed it without complaint, which was more than he could say about some soldiers he knew.

He needed to do better.

Vekele stood in the kitchen, unsure where to begin. He had very little in the way of fresh produce. When the new delivery came, he would ask for a greater variety, but that did not help him now.

The pantry had several types of packaged food, all providing enough vitamins and calories to sustain existence, but he doubted that would please Sarah.

He did not know why it was important to please the female. In his generosity, he provided water, sustenance, and shelter, in addition to medical care. She should be grateful for the gelatinous and nutritionally balanced rations he provided, even if unappealing.

Yet here he was in the overgrown kitchen garden, searching for anything edible. His actions made no sense.

Last fall, in an uncharacteristic fit of optimism, he cleared the beds and planted seedlings for a spring harvest. He was not a gardener and the small plot had fallen into neglect.

He found a raised bed of leafy greens that had survived his abandonment and grazing from wildlife. There was a vine of heavy gourds that sprawled across the ground, covering most of the garden. He collected the ones that were ripe and nearly ripe. He had no idea how to prepare it, but leaving it to rot seemed a waste. In addition, he found a few berries and vegetables that had escaped grazing from the local animals.

His harvest seemed pitifully small, but it was a start.

Carefully, he read the instructions on how to prepare a box of grains. While the grains boiled, he researched the best way to cook the gourds. The knives in the kitchen were insulting. Dull from neglect, he spent far too long bringing the blade back to acceptable sharpness. Chopping required that he hold his head at an uncomfortable angle. He felt ridiculous, head tilted and hunched over the cutting board.

Vekele paused, setting down the blade. If anyone were to see him, they would mock his weakness, and then… well, that was why he spent the last year in exile at Summerhall.

No. The female required sustenance, and that was more important than his ego.

He shook off any lingering insecurities and resumed the meal preparation. What did he care if he looked ridiculous? He was a prince. If any dared to mock him, they would suffer the consequences.

While he worked, he tried not to think about Baris requesting an update on the captive. He responded with vague assurances that he continued to interrogate Sarah Krasinski but had nothing of significance to report.

That was incorrect.

A network search of the Arcosian archives turned up a report on humans. A classified Reilen document, it was decades out of date, perhaps even a century. How it came to be in the archives, he would not speculate. His people had once been great traders of resources, information being the most valuable resource. Some noble ancestor believed that if Reilen considered the dossier on humans important enough to be classified, then it was important enough to be in the royal archives.

Vekele wanted to thank that unknown ancestor, as that report provided the bulk of all known information about Earth and its humans. Nothing in the report contradicted what Sarah had told him. Earth was primitive. Perhaps not as technologically backward as when Reilen surveyed the planet, but the report was outdated.

The most tantalizing bit of information came from Duras, a footnote in a report. Apparently, humans were genetically compatible. The Reilen report only hinted at this, but the Duras report contained an anecdote of a Khargal soldier stranded on Earth who took a human mate and had offspring.

Vekele did not want to share any of this information with Baris. Not yet.

Not until he understood why it affected him so, why it planted the seductive idea in his mind of taking Sarah Krasinski of Earth as his mate.

She had and lost a mate, she told him. Years had passed, but he heard the pain in her voice as she talked about her lost mate. There would be no room in her heart for another.

Entertaining such thoughts was the height of foolishness. Vekele had spoken true when he said that the king would select his mate. He expected a political match and nothing more.

The knife thunked against the cutting board with too much force, releasing a small amount of frustration.

Until he found Sarah in the ruins of Miria, he had accepted the necessity of a political mating. He was a prince. He had a duty to the king, the family, and the stability of the kingdom.

How could he refuse his king? After all, Baris would not ask Vekele to do something he himself was unwilling to do. His brother had been negotiating a peace treaty to unite two warring Shadowmark and Starshade families together in marriage. Did Baris have affection for his mate? Irrelevant.

As irrelevant as Vekele's own wants and desires.

And he wanted with such intensity that it baffled him.

He wanted to savor every inch of her curves and explore their *compatibility*. Her proportions were strange, shorter, and broader than the average Arcosian. Her hips were wide, ideal for gripping hard while he drove his cock into her. He wanted to see that: her red hair spilled across the bed, a moan on her lips, and ecstasy on her odd human face.

He wanted to taste her, to savor every part of her.

Desire, a sensation he had not felt in so long, sparked and flared within him. She had the royal mark on her. She was made for him. The court and nobility might be skeptical of such a mating, but no one would dare question him. He was still a prince. He could persuade Baris to allow the mating...

No. It would be wrong.

The power imbalance between them soured the idea. She depended on him for her survival. If she agreed to anything, he could never shake the feeling of coercion.

Not while she was chained to his bed.

Power imbalance would always be an issue. Potential partners saw his title and status first, Vekele as a male second, if they ever really saw him at all. He found it easier to be alone than to deal with the complications of physical or romantic relationships. Now...

Now his world had been shaken by this human.

Despite his glares and grumbles, he enjoyed listening to Sarah. He liked her questions, even if he had no answer for them. She commandeered every conversation. Watching her mind leap from subject to subject was dizzying. Physically, he found her attractive, but her intellect proved far more compelling. Good humor and mirth bubbled up from within her, her joy flowing from an endless well. He wanted to guzzle that jubilation straight from the source, to gorge himself until he was no longer parched and thirsting.

A power imbalance existed between them, with her in command.

Perhaps she was an agent sent to sow discord. The qualities that compelled him were nothing more than an illusion. He did not want it to be true, but acknowledged that risk. He needed to be cautious with the female. He needed to keep his head. He definitely needed to keep her confined to Summerhall until he was sure of her motives.

The kitchen was too warm, he used too many dishes, and the sizable pile of greens had cooked down to a handful of mush.

He considered the bowl of mixed greens and grains, unsure if she would find the taste bland or the texture disturbing. His best effort did not look appetizing, but it would have to do.

Carefully, he carried the tray into the bedroom and balanced it as he opened the door. The sensors on the doors ceased working long ago and no longer opened as one approached.

Sarah sat by the window, feet tucked up underneath her, and stared out at the gardens. Light pooled around the chair and shadows grew as the sun set. The golden chain glinted in the light.

She turned and smiled.

At him.

It was foolish to feel a flutter of vanity, that she liked his face. She had been delirious. Confused. No doubt her vision had been impaired. Her words held no importance.

And yet…

"Food," he said, dropping the tray to the table because he did not care, and he was not acting foolishly over the female who may or may not like his face.

The entire situation was frustrating.

"I can see that," she said, sitting at the table. With her hands folded in her lap, she looked at him expectantly.

Vekele stood still, his back rigid. "Eat," he ordered.

"You gonna sit down and join me? Are we pretending that's a thing we don't do?" she asked.

He did not huff as he sat. He retained his dignity. He was a *prince*.

She took a spoonful of the grains. He did not watch her, waiting for her reaction. Dignity, prince, and so forth.

"It's good," she said. "It's got a consistency like risotto."

He released the breath he did not realize he had held.

He dipped his head, focusing on his own bowl and definitely not smiling.

CHAPTER SEVEN

SARAH

Sarah woke to complete darkness. Moonlight through windows could not pierce the shadows in the room. Her heart raced from a half-remembered dream.

I was running through the forest.

The sensation of miserable rain and searching for a lost someone lingered.

Rain pounded against the windows. Thunder rumbled. The storm must have wormed its way into her dream.

She heard something. Vekele's unnamed karu prowling in the dark? She held her breath, listening to the sounds of the house and the storm.

"Vekele?" she whispered. He slept on the fainting couch, or whatever fancy people called it, but the couch was empty.

No response. She was alone.

Gradually, the light came back, or her eyes adjusted to the dark. Moonlight collected in faint pools by the windows.

She stumbled into the bathroom, filling a glass of water from the tap. The lights flickered on.

In the mirror, a black-eyed reflection of herself stared back. Inky black pools spread from her eyes like spidery veins of decay.

The glass fell to the floor, shattering. Water and glass shards flowed around her bare feet.

"What is the matter?" Vekele shoved his way into the room.

"I—" She pointed to the mirror. Her eyes were her normal brown. She didn't know how to explain what she saw moments before. "Nothing. I'm half-asleep. Where were you?"

"Patrol. I cannot constantly be at your side in case you have unpleasant dreams," he said, sounding annoyed.

"Yeah, well—" She bit back her retort because he was right. "Sorry for the mess."

She crouched down to pick up the broken glass.

"Leave it. You will injure yourself."

"I'm perfectly capable."

"Must you always argue?" he muttered. That was all the warning she had before he scooped her up like a sack of potatoes and carried her out of the bathroom.

She wasn't upset about the whole sack of potatoes thing because being carried was kind of nice.

He sat her on the edge of the bed and lifted her chin toward the light. He turned her head from side to side, frowning.

"What?" she asked.

"It is nothing."

"Yeah, I'm not buying that. It's the parasite, isn't it? It's in my eyes." Just the thought of it made her want to claw at her face to get it out.

"I cannot say." He stepped back, putting distance between them.

She groaned. "You're making it worse. Tell me."

"I cannot say because I am not a medic. He will examine you tomorrow. Now, sleep." He punched the pillows on the couch and laid down.

Fat chance she'd be able to sleep now.

VEKELE DREW the curtains back with enough force to create a cloud of dust.

"What's happening?" Sarah asked between coughs. The unnerving feeling from last night still lingered. She didn't feel like herself. Unsettled. Restless. Still searching in the forest for something lost.

He pressed his thumb against a black panel on the window frame, and a locking mechanism groaned as it released.

"Your mental and physical stimulation is inadequate. You will walk the grounds for one hour," he said, pushing open the window. Cool air flooded in, still sweet and refreshing from last night's storm. It carried flowery scents from the garden and damp earth.

"Outside? Seriously?" Sarah jumped off the bed. "I need shoes."

"Eat. The medic will be here shortly to examine you," he said, pointing to the tray on the table.

Sarah gulped down the smoothie and the nutritionally sound but gross jello without tasting them. As quickly as she could, she washed her face, brushed her hair, and dressed. A pair of shoes that weren't there yesterday waited in the wardrobe.

An excited giddiness bubbled and fizzed inside her at the possibility of going outside. Was this how Stockholm Syndrome started? Fresh air and sunshine were things she'd actively avoided back home, but the chance to get out of this damn room made her feel like a kid on Christmas morning.

"There is something I must do first." He motioned for her to sit and crouched at her feet. "I must remove this."

He gripped the heel of her foot, and his thumb brushed over her ankle. Her skin tingled where they touched, like something inside her needed out. He held her foot for a moment too long, and Sarah sucked in a breath. Skin warmed from contact. Her whole body warmed, too hot for the room.

This felt intimate, more than simply inspecting her ankle for damage from the chain.

"Is something wrong?" she asked.

"No," he answered quickly, voice rough.

The chain fell away, though the band remained.

He glanced up, head held at that awkward angle that meant he was looking directly at her. His eyes were black. All four of them. Tendrils of pitch-black ink moved under his skin, heading toward his eyes.

"Oh," she said, voice no louder than a whisper.

He dropped her foot like it scalded him. He scrubbed a hand over his face and the black tendrils retreated. An angry expression flickered across his face, shuttering whatever vulnerability he had—but honestly, he had a strong resting bastard face game, so it was difficult to tell if he was genuinely angry or bored.

"What was that?" she asked.

"The symbiote that lives in me."

"Is that… is that what's in me?" She remembered the sleepy, horrific reflection in the mirror. "You said it was a parasite infection."

"In you, it is an infection, yes. My body has bonded with the organism, and we have a symbiotic relationship."

She wanted to know more, but his tone made it clear he wasn't in a talkative mood.

Focus on the positive. The chain was gone.

"Thanks," she said. Rubbing her ankle, she ran a finger under the band to massage the skin. The area around her ankle seemed bruised, but that had to be a trick of the light. The discoloration faded when she tried to get a better look.

She considered making a smartass remark about Vekele failing to make her promise not to escape, but not with that look on his face. He had shown her kindness. She should do the same.

"Do not give me gratitude for removing the chain. You are still my captive," he said.

There he was, her arrogant alien prince.

He continued, "The band is connected to the house's security system. It will track your location. You are free to walk the grounds, but you will not be able to cross the boundary. The band will vibrate as a warning. If you attempt to escape, you will be restrained until I retrieve you."

"Stay in the yard. Got it," she said, opening the wardrobe to retrieve the shoes.

The window opened directly onto the lawn. Outside, she tilted her head back to savor the warm sunlight.

Grass and weeds threatened to overtake a crushed gravel path, but enough remained for Sarah to figure out where it was. She followed rows of overgrown flower beds. Once tidy shrubbery burst from the beds. Flowers were a wild riot of color. Insects buzzed through the air, flitting from flower to flower and ignoring her.

Placed strategically, stone benches offered a seat in a shade and an opportunity to appreciate the view. She paused to sit and take inventory. Other than stiffness, she didn't hurt. Chalk it up to advanced alien medicine.

The garden had once been something spectacular. Even in its neglected state, it remained stunning. Rather compact, the garden sat near the house. On the north side, the lawn gently sloped away toward the dense forest.

Sweat collected in the small of her back. Despite the heat, she carried on exploring. After all, she'd be just as hot inside as she was out. When Vekele locked her back in, she'd take a bath.

The south lawn held a pond and a small domed pavilion. In the center of the pond, the remains of a disused fountain sat partially submerged. Intrigued, Sarah skirted around the pond and made her way to the structure.

The pavilion sat right at the water's edge. The stone structure was cool, even in the summer heat. Just beyond, the forest crowded close. This must have been near the boundary of the property. Not wanting to test the ankle band or the security system, she was perfectly content to sit in the pavilion. If Vekele was watching — and she absolutely believed he was—she wanted to prove that she was trustworthy.

"Totally not escaping," she said, just in case the ankle band had a mic as well as a tracker.

Something shifting in the shadows of the trees caught her attention. A glint of light? The hint of another forgotten building? Rich people did that, right? Built life-size dollhouses simply for the aesthetics and called them follies.

The shadows moved again. The hair on the back of her neck stood on end. She took a self-defense class a long, long time ago. The only thing she remembered was that the instructor said to listen to your gut. If something felt wrong, it was wrong. Her brain hadn't processed what her subconscious already knew.

It was too quiet, with a complete lack of birdsong or insects buzzing by.

This was wrong. She needed to get out of here.

A growl came from the tree line. The shadows under the trees elongated and grew denser, like they drained the day of sunlight.

Sarah carefully climbed down the pavilion steps, facing the forest. Turning her back to whatever was out there seemed like a seriously bad idea.

A beast stepped forward. The form had the same familiar shape as the monster that attacked her in the temple. Smoke rolled off its back.

No, not smoke. Shadows. They boiled and writhed, pitch black and snaking across the lawn toward her.

Her palms itched. Sarah flexed her fingers, wanting to run, but all she could do was stare at the beast. Triangular ears stood tall over its head, proving that the game pieces had not been stylized.

A tendril brushed against her leg, like a question. *Yes? Yes, yes, yes.*

The light dimmed.

A shiver went through her, breaking whatever hold the creature had.

She ran.

It chased.

Sure, in retrospect, running from monsters seemed like a bad idea. They lived with the hunt and she did not do cardio. At all. Ever. Cutting across the lawn toward the house seemed like the fastest way to get herself eaten. In the trees, she had a chance of hiding.

She veered to the left, toward the trees. The band at her ankle vibrated in warning. It started as a gentle hum, growing stronger once she reached the trees.

Good. Let the security system snitch on her to Vekele.

She tripped over a root, falling to her knees, but picked herself back up and kept running. Branches whipped against her skin. She held up her arms to protect her face. Fabric snagged and tore. A small part of her brain —the part not screaming in terror—wondered why she wasn't puking her guts up right now. She panted and her legs burned, but it was a mild discomfort. She should have sidestitches and be wheezing. The last time she ran for anything had been in high school, a decade ago.

The light gradually increased, even under the canopy of the trees. She darted from one puddle of light to another, just in case the creature was averse to sunlight like a vampire. Yes, that made no sense, but whatever. Her gut said to aim for the light, and she wasn't going to second-guess instinct. That luxury could wait until she wasn't running for her life.

She glanced over her shoulder, not spotting the beast.

She stopped, panting, with her hands on her hips. Her heart pounded in her ears, drowning out any other sounds. She needed to be quiet, but it was so hard when she gasped for breath.

She waited for the beast to catch up, but nothing happened. As the seconds rolled by and nothing happened, she relaxed.

It worked. She lost the—

Something grabbed her by the ankle, knocking her off her feet. A yelp slipped from her lips. An unseen force pulled her roughly along the forest floor. She twisted and kicked, trying to break free. Her shirt snagged on a rock, ripping the fabric, and slicing into her. Her back burned as she was scraped raw, and she shouted in pain. She felt every stick, rock, and tree root.

Finally, she came to rest against a large stone pillar. Circles bored through the stone in a decorative pattern that probably meant something. A brand name, perhaps. *Home Defense 3000 Pro* or *Lurker in the Woods Ultra.*

Sarah groaned. Everything hurt. Her right foot hung off the pillar, attached by a familiar gold chain, only this one was short and not the ever-expanding chain from the house. She felt like a rabbit caught in a snare.

Worse. A dumb bunny who ran from a wolf straight into a trap.

She kicked at the pillar, trying to push off with her foot to snap the chain. No joy. The chain was only a few inches long and kept her foot elevated. She was stuck on her back until Vekele freed her.

Growling sounded from the shadows.

Her stomach sank. This was so much worse. Now she was bleeding and tied to a pillar, basically a monster buffet.

The beast stepped forward.

"Hey," she said, twisting her head to get a better view. From her perspective, the beast's paws were huge. "You probably wanna eat, but that's a bad idea. I like junk food, so I'm full of preservatives."

The paws crept closer. Inky black pools spread across the ground, twisting through leaves and grass, right toward her.

VEKELE

He followed the female.

For surveillance. Not that he wanted to watch her as she explored the grounds or wanted to see the way the sunlight picked out golden highlights in her hair. Because that was behavior reserved for the young and foolish.

Surveillance.

If he repeated that enough, he would believe his lie.

Baris' patience neared an end, and he demanded an update on the female. Vekele did not believe the female to be a spy or even an agent sent to sow discord and chaos. He believed the ludicrous story of her communication device opening a portal, despite being unable to replicate that phenomenon with the contraption. The reports he read claimed human tech was not advanced, but the reports were ancient in terms of intelligence. He would disregard them entirely if he had any other information about humans.

Sarah's wanderings through Summerhall's ground churned up Vekele's memories. This place had been his home and his prison for most of his adolescence. He knew every inch of the house and had explored the grounds. Summerhall kept no secrets from him. He wanted to show her the initials carved into a retaining wall, left by a long-dead ancestor. When she paused under a large tree, he bit back the urge to tell the story of how Baris pushed him from the tree, and he broke his arm.

She headed to the small pond on the edge of the boundary. If she strayed too close to the boundary, the security system would detain her. She could not enjoy the experience. He knew. The band she wore had been his.

Several times, too often to count, he tested the security system and searched for weak points in the boundary. Each time, his efforts ended with him on his back, his foot chained to a pillar.

The system his uncle designed was crude but effective.

Sarah's posture changed. She stiffened, as if frightened.

Vekele stepped back, gathering a shadow to cloak himself. Stalking her in the bright light of day had been a mistake.

She bolted. Not toward the house, toward safety, but deeper into the trees.

A shadowy creature followed. It was small, but he recognized a void beast.

"Track them," he said to the karu. The words had barely left his lips before she took flight.

Wings of darkness and shifting shadow erupted from his back. They did him no good, only hindering him as he moved through the trees. Stealth was impossible and speed impractical. Frustration grew that Sarah would choose to run into the dense trees rather than out into the open where he could shield her. He latched onto that frustration. As long as her choices irritated him, he could ignore the gnawing worry.

Sarah was not a warrior. While she had a strong spirit and a stronger will, her body was fragile. She had already been injured. If she were injured again while under his care, the medic would give him such a lashing—and he would deserve every word.

A yelp pierced through the silence. That would be the perimeter defense activating. He ran toward the sound, ignoring the branches that battered against his wings.

He broke into a clearing.

The void beast sat directly on Sarah's chest, gnawing on her face. It was a horrible sight. She writhed on the ground in obvious agony. Why she giggled instead of screamed had to be a human defect, some strange coping mechanism.

He was too late.

"Beast!" He surged forward.

The beast looked up and snarled.

"It's cool. You're freaking him out," Sarah said.

The beast resumed licking her face. She laughed. *Laughed.*

Nothing made sense.

CHAPTER EIGHT

SARAH

"Sarah, remain still," Vekele said, his voice calm. Too calm, which did not make her feel calm.

"Tell me what's going on," she said, decidedly not calm. The puppy sitting on her did not like her tone and licked her face. It felt like sandpaper. Wet, wiggly sandpaper.

"I have two pieces of information that will seem conflicting," he said, inching closer.

The puppy growled a warning, and Sarah felt it resonate with her.

"He doesn't like you," she said.

"I am aware."

A nervous laugh bubbled up in her throat. That grabbed the puppy's attention. He turned his eyes to her, four pools of inky darkness.

Half the monster's features said massive danger cat, such as the slim build and the triangular ears. The other half, especially the dog-shaped muzzle full of extra sharp bitey bits, was solidly wolf. Why her brain looked at a four-eyed shadowy monster with paws and enough teeth to make a shark jealous and thought *puppy*, she had no idea. She'd question it later.

"Hey, hey," she said in a soothing tone. "It's cool. I like Vekele. He's a friend."

She held up a hand. The puppy sniffed it, then bumped his head against her palm. His soft fur had a wispy texture, like fluffy. When it became apparent that the puppy wasn't going to tear her throat out or lunge at Vekele, she asked, "What's your conflicting information?"

"You no longer have a parasitic infection," he said.

"That's good."

"You have been elevated to an aristocrat."

"That's very good." Though she didn't know how or why.

"You are now in a symbiotic relationship with the parasite."

"That's… less good. Did you just good news, bad news me? Hey, your body is no longer fighting the parasite. They're totally chill roommates now." Her voice rose in pitch, growing more stressed.

The puppy did not like this and blamed Vekele. He snarled and snapped in warning. She made shushing noises. Eventually, the puppy settled down, resting his head on his paws.

"You are bonded to the void beast," Vekele said, like that clarified anything.

"Like you and your karu?"

"Yes."

The puppy gazed at her with black, black eyes.

Bonded. It felt unreal, but also, yeah. She could believe it. Something inside her felt connected, like how she knew the puppy was tired and so glad he found her. She got the impression of pack and home and together.

"He used to have many. Now he has me," she said. The karu squawked. "Us," she corrected.

That felt right. They were a pack together. Different, but the same.

"But how?" she asked. "I thought you did a sacred quest for your bond."

"A sacrifice of salt and blood," Vekele said, again, as if that clarified anything. "The void beasts and karu carry the same organism. The karu pair bond. The beasts form a pack. You were infected by the pack that attacked you."

Sarah wanted to know why he called it a parasite when it was in her, but when he spoke about himself, it was an organism.

"You didn't mention this would happen. You said the infection would clear."

"Bonding with the beats is rare because the pack can resist the bond." His voice sounded... she wasn't sure. Embarrassed that he'd been wrong? Remorseful? It was hard to tell without looking at him, but she didn't want to take her eyes off the puppy, just in case he decided to eat her face.

"You said you killed the pack," she said.

"I was incorrect. One member survived."

"How does any of this make me an aristocrat?"

"Those who are bonded are elevated to the status. It is one of the oldest customs on Arcos. All noble families have their roots in a bond, though not all members of the house are bonded."

Okay, that was strange. Being elevated in status over something she accidentally did seemed marginally better than being born into wealth or rank. Barely. She'd worry about it later.

Carefully, she scratched behind the puppy's ear. He closed his eyes—all four—in pleasure. His tail beat hard enough against her raised leg, the one caught in the trap, to feel like being beaten with a stick.

"He's just a baby. I must have gotten too close to their den. They were protecting him," she said. Sorrow washed through her that she dropped on top of a pack and inadvertently caused their demise. It wasn't anyone's fault, and the injustice of it brought tears to her eyes.

The puppy echoed back feelings of being alone and sad.

"How far did he travel to get here? It's been, what, a week? Two?"

The puppy had to be old enough to find food, but he was far from an adult. Granted, during her one experience with full -grown void beasts, she hadn't been taking notes. She guessed the puppy was about the size of a three-month-old Labrador.

"Twelve days. It is not an inconsiderable journey."

The puppy huffed.

"Agreed," she muttered. "You hungry? Of course you are. A not -inconsiderable journey really takes it out of you."

"Do not speak to it."

"What? You talk to your bird all the time."

"It is young. We can sever the bond."

The puppy growled.

"Same," she agreed, stroking his head to calm him. "Nothing is being severed."

She flopped around, trying to roll to one side enough to look at Vekele. The best she could get was a view of his shoes. "This adventure sucks. So far, it's been running for my life or being chained to things."

She shook her foot for emphasis.

"Do not disturb the void beast," he said, approaching cautiously.

The puppy lifted its head and flashed its teeth in warning.

Vekele stepped back, hands up to indicate his lack of weapons if the puppy cared for such things.

"Yeah, maybe you should try not upsetting him," she retorted back.

"Now is not the time for jests."

"I dunno. You ever heard of dark humor? Seems like having a murdery shadow puppy sitting on my chest is a pretty good time to crack some jokes."

"I do not understand you," he said.

"Same."

VEKELE

Eventually, the beast allowed him to approach the security terminal. The karu perched on the pillar, watching as he negotiated in small increments with the beast. Releasing Sarah was as simple as pressing his thumb to the scanner. Reaching the security pylon took a quarter of an hour.

Once the chain released, he grabbed her by the elbow and pulled her to her feet. The beast yipped and growled, but Vekele ignored it. He turned Sarah around, looking for injury. Other than scrapes on her back and arms, she was unharmed.

Relieved, he placed his hand on the back of her neck and pressed his forehead to hers. This close, he relished the scent of crushed grass, fresh earth, and sweat on her skin, all the aromas of being alive.

Then, only then, did he relax enough to retract his wings.

"Your eyes," she said.

"It is nothing." Releasing his grip on the shadows within himself proved more difficult than he antici- pated. This female attracted trouble. He needed to be ready to protect her.

Sarah scooped up the beast, cradling it in her arms. It was too big to hold and squirmed until she set it down. Bits of leaves and grass clung to her clothing and hair, giving her the appearance of a wild forest spirit.

Despite his appreciation for the aesthetic charm of her current appearance, he plucked a stray leaf from her hair.

"The medic will be here shortly," he said. If the bond could be severed, Harol would know.

"We're not severing the bond," she said, sensing his thoughts. "Traveler is hungry. Feed us."

"Do not name the beast," he said, marching back to the house. The karu landed on his shoulder, digging her talons in.

She considered the beast at her side, reaching down to touch his head—*its head*. Her soft ways were corrupting him.

"Fine, not that name, but he has a name. I'll find it," she said.

"Beasts do not have names."

"Right, just like Pitch on your shoulder does not have a name."

The karu responded with pleasure. Pitch was a good name. She liked it.

Dammit all.

In the kitchen, he ordered her to sit at the work table. She twisted her head around to take in the room.

"Two eyes are so inefficient. I am amazed you see anything at all," he said. He opened the cooling unit, freshly stocked with a delivery that morning. His food preparation skills were unremarkable, but he could put together something palatable. He did not know what the beast would consume. Innocents and hatchlings, presumably.

"You seem to get by with two," she said.

He tensed, holding onto the door of the cooling unit. Her words had been harsh but had not been spoke with malice.

"You noticed," he said. Of course Sarah noticed. She noticed everything he wished to keep hidden. He did not understand the reason he withheld that information from her. Perhaps he did not wish for her to regard him as less capable.

Foolishness.

"Sorry," she said. "Is that another thing we're not supposed to talk about? I can't tell. You have so many rules."

"I do not have *so many* rules. Two. Two rules, and you violated one today. You were not to leave the house's grounds."

"I was being chased! I was scared." She tightened her hold on the beast. "Scout's just a baby. He didn't know he was scaring me."

The beast wiggled in her arms. It was foolish to feel jealous of the creature.

"Its name is not Scout."

"Yeah, that's not badass enough. You're little now, but you're gonna be a big old badass when you grow up." She directed the last half of the statement to the beast, who squirmed in delight.

Pitch twittered in amusement.

"Not you too," he muttered to the karu.

Pitch was not a dignified name. Another chirp. Pitch disagreed and sent a strong impression of kicking a spoiled egg out of the nest.

He leveled a finger at Pitch. "Traitor," he said.

Sarah chattered at the beast while he worked. It was… pleasant. He did not appreciate having the beast in his home. Stars only knew what vermin it carried. It needed a bath, and Sarah's injuries, while not threatening, needed to be cleaned. Until both beast and female were fed, Vekele would be unable to do either.

She filled the kitchen with light and mirth. His paltry contribution of barely palatable food did not seem enough. He should have allowed her access to other parts of the house. She made the silence bearable.

He would even tolerate the beast once it had been deloused. Harol had warned him that a bond was a possibility. He had not listened.

Vekele failed to do many things.

He set a plate in front of her. It was a simple meal with a filet of protein and steamed vegetables.

"Thank you. It smells wonderful," she said.

"Do not lie to spare my feelings."

"I'm being polite." She cut the protein into strips, feeding the beast before herself.

He sat opposite her at the table, ignoring his plate as he watched her feed the beast. She had no fear of the creature, despite being severely injured by its pack.

"You're not eating?" she asked.

He took a bite, chewing with mock enthusiasm.

"I like you, Prince Vekele. You're full of spite."

He snorted. Pitch made a similar noise. It was not spite that people claimed filled him.

"I should have told you about the potential for the bond," he said, turning to see her better. "You can speak Arcosian. Clearly, some part of the bond took root early. Then you would not have been frightened and you would not have been injured."

Sarah blinked. One. Two. The beast mimicked. Left. Right. It was unnerving.

"Language is part of the bond? I thought you put an implant in my head or something." She frowned. "It's weird that I never thought to ask. Why didn't I ask?"

The question sounded as if it was directed to herself. Still, he answered. "You were feverish. Your body has gone through a transformation that many do not survive. An implant was a reasonable assumption. I initially scanned you for such a device."

Her head bobbed up and down, a gesture he recognized as agreement. "You need to tell me this sort of stuff."

"I did not—"

"Know if you could trust me, right," she said, speaking over him. No one had ever dared speak over him, but he did not mind. Her audacity amused him. "But I needed to know that. Going forward, please share with me. I'm not asking for state secrets, but the basics that I need to know. Like everything about this bond."

Sarah stroked the beast while she spoke. The beast stared at Vekele and licked his chops. Again, he was not jealous of the smug little creature.

"Agreed," he said. "I know little of the bonds with a void beast. They are rare enough to be thought impossible."

She hummed. "How about wings? Am I going to grow wings?"

"Unlikely. Bond abilities manifest differently. Wings are common with the karu."

"Can you fly?"

"No. They are mainly defensive." In the past, he had glided from heights, but it was a difficult maneuver. "You will share senses with the void beast."

"Thoughts? Like a telepathic link?"

"Impressions and emotions. The older the creature, the more complex the thoughts. A hatchling such as him, you can expect base emotions."

"Hungry. Tired. Alone," she said, repeating what she already sensed.

"In time, the bond will strengthen. You will develop the ability to manipulate shadow and light." He held up a hand to demonstrate, letting the shadows swallow up the light until only a single bulb over the table provided illumination.

"That is cool."

He should not preen at such praise, but as he recalled the shadows with a thought, his chin lifted ever so slightly in delight. Pitch echoed the praise with warmth and affection for her hatchling.

"I will have to inform the king of this development," he said.

The beast in her lap gave a sleepy whine. It jumped to the floor and circled her chair before settling down beneath it. Its legs and tail poked out from underneath.

"You make that sound like a bad thing," she said.

Pitch perched on the back of his chair. Absently, he fed the berries from his plate to her, one by one.

"It is complicated, but you must know this—I am blind in my front eyes. Your observation was correct." He waited for sympathy, an empty platitude about still being capable or incorrect wisdom that his other senses would compensate for the loss. She said nothing, allowing him to explain his condition without those burdens. "A year ago, I was attacked. Acid was thrown in my face. I lost almost all my vision. The medics say I may regain some vision in time, but currently, it is only vague shapes and some color."

"Is that why your front eyes are cloudy?" she asked.

"Presumably. My medic tells me it is mostly healed. I have spent the last year here, recovering."

"Thank you for sharing that with me."

He disliked exposing his vulnerabilities, but she needed to understand. He said, "The king is my brother. He may have ordered the attack on me. I cannot be certain."

"Oh." For once, she had no words.

"Politics hold no interest for me, but the spiders spinning their webs at court do not care for my desires. I have... I had a successful military career. If I wanted to seize the throne from my brother, I would have the backing of the military. It is only logical that Baris would remove me as a threat." Suspicions he had not dared to utter for a year tumbled out of him. He felt relieved, like a poison had been purged.

"This is your brother? Would he do that?"

He did not wish to explain the last century of brutal political maneuvering to gain the throne. "There is no room for sentimentality in politics. If Baris did not give the order, then someone took it upon themselves to remove a potential threat. Or perhaps the goal was to sow mistrust between us? It does not matter."

"Agree to disagree there," she said, picking at the remaining berries on her plate. She tossed one to Pitch, who snatched it midair. Another went to the void beast under her chair. "So you're telling me all this because..."

"Because you will be a tool or a symbol. Perhaps both. You bear the royal mark. You arrived at a holy site. You bonded with a void beast."

"Coincidence."

"One is a coincidence. Two is chance. Three could be fate, if that is the message the king wishes to send."

Separately, they were nothing. Together, they were a tool.

"Well, that's a lot to take in," she said. "Thank you for explaining it to me. It can't be nice badmouthing your brother."

Badmouthing. She had such an unpolished way with words. The predators that roosted at the court would circle her, looking for any weakness. Sarah would shine like a rough gem at court or crumble under pressure.

The security system alerted him to the medic's arrival.

He knew two things with certainty: Harol would pluck the feathers from his back for endangering Sarah, and he would protect her from anyone who would harm her, including the king.

SARAH

The medic fussed over the road rash on her back and then fussed at Vekele for not cleaning the wounds immediately. The antiseptic stung, but the numbing agent erased any discomfort. At no point did anyone mention severing the bond.

The medic then declared her "as well as can be expected" and gave strict orders not to be dragged through the forest by her ankles or fall through ceilings.

Basically, no fun at all.

"It's not like I did either on purpose," she said, brushing out the puppy. Vekele had set up a tub in the small yard just outside the kitchen. The puppy didn't like the water, but he enjoyed having the soap massaged into his fur. More water ended up on her than on him, but she didn't mind. "You smell good... Cerberus? No. Don't give me that look. It's a classic name."

Talking kept the puppy calm enough to rinse off and brush out. Vekele lurked at the edges, never intruding but nearby if the puppy suddenly attacked. For all his growling and snarling at Vekele, he wouldn't attack. She knew that. They were pack now.

"I like him," she said, keeping her voice soft and soothing. "He's taken good care of me. We can trust him."

She liked Vekele for more reasons than that, but that had been the start. He used his body as a shield to protect her in the temple. At the time, she'd been too scared to appreciate the feel of his lean form against hers. He was gorgeous: tall, dark, and elven. That attitude, though, was an acquired taste. Still, her heart skipped a beat when his lips twitched with a smile that he was too regal and proud to display.

He listened to her. He noticed what foods she liked. And if he didn't think she noticed the way he pretended to read while listening to every silly word she said to the puppy, he was fooling himself.

And the way his eyes went black when he was in badass mode, with wings outstretched like a dark angel…

Wow. That was super-hot, and it was super inappropriate for her to be objectifying him like that, but wow. It should have been terrifying, but it was the sexiest thing she'd ever seen.

Sarah looked over her shoulder at Vekele lounging on the steps outside the kitchen doorway. Late afternoon sunlight picked out silvery strands in his hair. The sleeves of his shirt were rolled up, exposing his forearms. Amazing how that look was universally attractive.

He glanced up and she looked away quickly, pretending that she hadn't been checking him out.

The puppy pushed his nose against her hand. His opinions on Vekele were far less complicated. No trust. Tolerate only for pack.

"For our pack?" Such a strange concept to wrap her head around.

She scratched behind the puppy's ears, giving him her undivided attention. Finally dried, his fur was silky soft but had the odd habit of wanting to stand on end and wave, as if caught in a breeze. Majestic? Sure. Creepy? Definitely.

"I didn't know about your family. I'm sorry about what happened to them," she said. "I didn't know. I just fell. They were protecting you." The bond connecting them felt tenuous, a flimsy thing made more of optimism and wishful thinking than fact. She wanted to believe that he understood her and kept talking, if only to process her thoughts.

Twelve days. She'd been gone for twelve days. She knew days had passed, but she hadn't counted. They blurred together.

The milk's gone bad, and the tomatoes will be rotten.

She didn't know why her first thought was of expiring food in her fridge, but there it was. How long before people realized she was gone? She hadn't been friendly with any of her neighbors, and she didn't live anywhere near her friends. That had been the point of moving away, to escape memories.

She called her mother once a month. Seraphina wouldn't notice anything amiss for a few weeks.

Trisha would know something happened. When Sarah didn't show up for drinks, she'd drop by the apartment. Most likely to yell at Sarah for standing her up and not having the decency to cancel via text.

The bookstore would call when she didn't show up for her shift. If her manager would be bothered to go to her apartment to check on her, she had no idea.

She couldn't have been the only person this happened to. Everyone had a phone, right? There were more phones than people on Earth. How many didn't get the update? Even if less than one percent of phones had the glitch, it was a staggering amount.

How long before anyone noticed she was gone?

Trisha, her mother, and her boss. Maybe.

That was sad. She hadn't always been so isolated, but apparently, she did a better job at hiding from the world than she expected.

The puppy nosed at the hand holding the brush. She stopped brushing.

"Sorry, too busy wallowing in my misery," she said. "I was just thinking about home. My family's gone too."

There. A spark, a cool silvery burst that felt like reassurance, like a promise. Not a direct thought, but an impression of one, like understanding body language.

"Thank you. I know you'll take care of me, Ghost. You've got all these teeth and such big paws." He was going to be huge, if the paws were any indication.

The puppy's tongue lolled out the side of his muzzle.

"Ghost? Do you like that one?" she asked. Yes, yes, yes came back to her. "Good. I like it, too."

Twelve days ago, her life was upended. She had no control over what would happen. Her fate depended on how useful she could be to the king.

———

Sᴀʀᴀʜ ᴋɴᴏᴄᴋᴇᴅ ᴛᴡɪᴄᴇ on the doorframe before entering. "So this is where you're hiding."

"I am not hiding. I am reading."

Vekele had sequestered himself away in the library, or what Sarah assumed to be the library. The bookshelves were a clue. He lounged in a chair; head tilted at an awkward angle over a book.

It was endearing and so, so hot.

She needed to get a grip on herself. This panting after the aloof, haughty prince was getting embarrassing. Vekele tolerated her. It didn't matter how attractive she found him, or that she giggled uncontrollably when he scowled. He was a prince. She worked in a bookstore.

As much as she wanted to convince herself that she fell through a portal into a Cinderella story, she didn't. It was, at best, Beauty and the Beast. The way Vekele looked at her, it was clear she was the beast.

"This room is nice." She trailed a finger along a shelf, marveling at the lack of dust.

After scrubbing Ghost clean, she'd wandered through the house, all bazillion rooms. As much as Vekele claimed it was a small summer house in the country, it was a palace. Disused, water -stained from a leaking roof, but still a palace. The only rooms that appeared to receive any regular cleaning were the kitchen, the bedroom, and the library.

That said a lot about Vekele's priorities, and she liked it.

"You are no longer confined to the bedroom. You may be anywhere in the house. You do not have to be here," he said, his tone crabby.

"I miss reading."

"You are free to read any book you please."

"But I can't actually read." She grabbed a slim book at random from a shelf. An indecipherable print filled the pages. Being illiterate sucked. "You know, I never really asked about the language thing."

"The organism that infected you can communicate with similar organisms in other hosts."

"So, magic."

"Not magic. Science." He paused, then added, "We can install a chip to allow you to read."

"Sounds good, and I like the way you said *we*." She winked, holding the book out to him. "Read this to me."

"This one?"

"Why not?"

"It is an economic analysis of the undue burden the outer planets pay in taxes."

"Yeah, maybe not that one. What are you reading?" She peered over his shoulder to get a look at the page. Worn at the edges, the book had seen a lot of use.

He snapped the book shut. "It is nothing."

"Is it porn?"

"No."

"It's okay if it is. I'm not judging. I once read a book where the hero had tentacles. Each one had a different purpose, and one was for reproduction, so it was a tenta-dick."

"No!" A bluish flush rose in his cheeks. "It is a collection of children's fables."

He spoke cautiously, expecting ridicule for reading children's stories. She asked, "Can you read aloud? That sounds interesting."

"It is." Another pause, as if debating what to say. "They are short and offer guidance on acceptable behavior. As a youth, I enjoyed them because the villains were always punished and the good were rewarded. Now, the stories take on a new meaning."

"We have stories that we tell children called fairy tales. It's mostly 'don't do this or you will die. ' 'Follow the rules or die. ' 'Don't wander into the forest or die.'"

"Is Earth so dangerous?" He frowned.

"Not really. I hardly ever get attacked by wolves when I wander through the forest."

He tilted his head, giving her that flat look that said he saw through her shit. "You tease me."

"A little." She held up a finger and thumb to indicate how little she teased. "But I would like to hear your story, please. I'm curious what an Arcosian children's fable is like."

"Very little wandering off to die," he said, voice dry.

She grinned and settled at the far end of the sofa. Ghost flopped down at her feet. Vekele cleared his throat, then read aloud. Eventually, she slid down to the floor and Ghost crawled into her lap. Vekele periodically touched the top of her head, as if verifying her location. His fingers stroked her hair with the barest whisper of contact.

She didn't even mind.

CHAPTER NINE

VEKELE

"This is inconvenient." Baris stood at the top of the lawn, arms folded over his chest. His karu hopped from his shoulder into a nearby tree. Both tilted their heads as they watched Sarah with the void beast. She threw a stick. The beast gave chase only to return with a different item, often not even a stick. Once he returned with an old leather shoe. Nonetheless, Sarah lavished praise on her bonded companion.

Vekele smothered the urge to smile.

"You were the one who sent me chasing after anomalies," he said.

"You do not have to sound so pleased."

Vekele tensed. He was not pleased. He was annoyed. The task had been a meaningless assignment given out of pity to get him out of his seclusion. It was insulting.

"It would have been less work for you if the assassins had done their job properly," he said. "Less torturous too."

Baris turned on him, drawing his shoulders back. While the same height as Vekele, Baris had an imposing figure granted by authority and the force of his will. His brother was gone, replaced by the king of Arcos.

"You think so little of me," the king said, his voice colder than the deepest winter night. "I have enough regard for you to send a properly skilled assassin and not bungle matters. If I wanted you dead, you would be dead."

The two brothers stared at each other. Just yesterday, he shared his doubt with Sarah. He disliked questioning Baris' motivation or loyalty. For years, Baris had been his only companion. They were brothers, yes, but also friends.

"I believe you," Vekele said.

"Apologize."

"I know you would look me in the eyes while plunging the dagger into my heart, as is honorable. Forgive me for implying otherwise."

Baris snorted. "You are fortunate that your impertinence amuses me."

"My insolence is sincere. That is my charm."

"Who told you that lie?"

Vekele's gaze drifted toward Sarah. He could not help himself. She burned like a bonfire, irresistible and inescapable.

"I see," Baris said.

"You see nothing," Vekele replied, a bit too quickly and a touch too emphatically.

Baris hummed, a noncommittal noise that indicated he did not wish to argue but wanted Vekele to know he was wrong.

"Nothing," Vekele repeated.

Baris' karu returned, clutching a ripe purple berry in his beak. Baris accepted the berry. The karu pecked gently at his ear until he consumed it. Satisfied, the karu took flight again.

"He thinks I am too thin," Baris said, explaining before Vekele could ask.

"You are," he said. Now that Vekele could see his brother in the strong daylight, he noticed how tired he appeared. Circles hung under his eyes, giving his face a weary look. Baris had always been the taller and broader brother, fitting the image of a warrior king, despite never having set foot on a battlefield. Now Baris seemed diminished. "I do not like it."

"A night of uninterrupted sleep is what I need, not food," Baris grumbled. Still, when the karu returned with another berry, he obediently ate it.

Vekele suspected his brother needed both sleep and food. "Surely you are not so important that the kingdom will fall apart without guidance for a few hours?"

"You have a way of keeping a male's ego humble," the king said, sounding amused. "Tell me about humans."

Vekele summarized the information he pulled from the archives.

"Yes, yes. I read all that. Tell me what you have learned from this human," Baris said.

Sarah's posture stiffened. No doubt she knew they discussed her. Ghost brought another stick, which she threw diligently into the trees. He darted off, shadows at his feet.

"Human technology has advanced. Sarah possessed a device that opened a portal and transported her here, but she is unaware of how it worked. I have examined the device and believe that it is malfunctioning."

"Send the device to Luca for analysis," Baris said.

"Consider it done," he said with a nod. Baris motioned for him to continue. "She claims her arrival was accidental. I am inclined to believe her. The royal mark is a coincidence."

"How did she acquire the mark? Is it recent?"

Vekele watched Sarah's reaction as he spoke. "It is not fresh. Old. Perhaps a handful of years. It is difficult to judge with her skin."

"Did you ask her?"

"Yes, I asked her," Vekele said, annoyance creeping into his voice. "She said it is based on an Earth animal that symbolizes wisdom."

Baris made a pleased noise. "And bonding with the void beast? It is difficult to believe the creature is tame."

Vekele was hesitant to call the void beast tame, but he was civil. *Civil-ish.* The void beast continued to growl when Vekele approached Sarah and watched him warily, as if Vekele were the beast.

"A fluke," he answered.

"Once is chance. Twice is a coincidence. Three times is a conspiracy," Baris said, nearly muttering.

"No one could orchestrate all those elements. What you are suggesting would be..." He refused to say *magic.* Eventually, he settled on, "Fantastical."

"Some would say the eyes of fate are watching," Baris said.

"I know which councilors would agree."

Ghost trotted out of the trees, carrying a small animal by the neck. It kicked and thrashed. He dropped it at Sarah's feet, and it bolted away. She jumped, startled.

Vekele huffed with amusement. Civil-ish, indeed.

"The wedding is a week away. No one can know about the human," Baris said. "If you bring her to court, it will disrupt everything. I get little enough sleep as it is."

"You suggest we continue to hide at Summerhall?"

"That is the sensible option. If knowledge of your human leaks, I can only do so much to control the situation," Baris said, exhaustion in his voice. "I could say her appearance is a blessing, a sign from the fates that we are on the correct path, but there are those on the council who will demand that a gift from the fates be married into the royal family. They will insist that no one less than the king will do."

Vekele knew exactly which councilors were traditionalists and would demand exactly that. "The treaty—"

Baris spoke over him. "Will not be signed until after the wedding. One unexpected *gift from the fates* can break the peace."

Sarah's posture stiffened, listening to their conversation.

Royal guards roamed the property. Vekele could not see them, but Baris would not have left the palace without at least two.

"How many know about her now? Us, your two guards, and the medic. Five. We can remain here for a week," Vekele said.

"And the person who delivers your supplies? Hikers in the forest? Media curious about the reclusive prince?" Baris listed people Vekele had not considered.

"They must be desperate for a story to stalk me."

"Too many people already know about her, and the potential for her discovery grows every day." Baris ran his hands through his hair.

His karu landed on his shoulder. Baris scratched behind the karu's head, then the karu preened his hair. As they seemed to be deep in conversation, Vekele did not disturb them. He gently tested his bond with Pitch, who supervised Ghost because he was a hatchling and certain to tumble out of the nest without her guidance.

Baris sighed. "We need to take control of this. The best way to do that is to bring her to court while we still control the story. Even if we plan it carefully, the treaty can still fall apart."

A valid point, but Vekele did not want to bring Sarah to the palace for a number of reasons. Parties opposed to the treaty would use her as a tool to break the peace. Mostly, Vekele did not want to share her. Sarah was his. His discovery. His human.

Sarah walked over, giving up the pretense that she had not overheard their discussion. He scowled. She raised her brows. "What? I can't be a part of the conversation that's about me? Let's just pretend that you made a weak argument about classified intel or something, and I ignore it. Agreed?"

Vekele tossed a glance to Baris. "It is faster if you agree now. She will not be deterred."

"So the big issue is keeping me a secret?" she asked, barely pausing for a response. "I think the solution is obvious: don't. Bring me to court and present me to the king, you, Your Highness. Make me a spectacle."

"Your Majesty, actually," Baris said, amusement in his tone.

"We have a saying on Earth: three can keep a secret if two are dead."

The king nodded. "Brutal but concise. We have a similar sentiment. The way to stop four tongues from wagging is to hold three in your hand."

Sarah shivered. "That's... effective."

Could no one see the flaw in this plan?

Vekele could no longer hold his tongue. Sarah proposed exactly what Baris said they could not do. "If I present Sarah to you at court, Councilor Raelle will demand that you marry her. The royal mark? The bond with the void beast? No one is more traditionalist than her. Negotiations will collapse, and the last year will have been for nothing."

Baris nodded in agreement. "Yes. Raelle is reliably traditionalist. She will demand a royal sacrifice, and I will sacrifice you."

It took a moment for the words to sink in. "Me? You want me to take Sarah as my mate?"

"For the peace of the kingdom," Baris said, his tone perfectly calm, seemingly unaware he had handed Vekele everything he secretly wanted.

Sarah would be his.

Baris addressed Sarah. "I only ask for a marriage of convenience. Once the treaty is signed, I will dissolve the union and you will be released. In return for your cooperation, I will find a way to send you back to Earth. Its location is known, though we currently lack a vessel capable of making such a journey. I will task my best engineer to reopen the portal with your device."

She barely paused to consider. "I'll do it."

SARAH

"Excuse us," Vekele said, grabbing Sarah's arm and marching her into the house. Once inside the bedroom —*don't look at the bed, don't look at the bed!*—he let go quickly, like touching her was a hardship.

Vekele, the noticer of everything, caught the nervous glance she gave the bed.

Shamefaced, Sarah scooted away, putting distance between them. Yeah, she couldn't volunteer to marry Vekele fast enough, despite Baris making it clear that it had to be *convincing* and that they would have to do their *duty*.

Like sharing a bed with the wildly attractive prince would be a hardship.

"Is this what you want?" Vekele asked.

"I said I'd do it."

He stepped closer, standing at her side. A hand landed on her shoulder, presumably to keep her from running away. "But is it what you want, Sarah Krasinski of Earth? To be mates? To share a bed? Share our bodies? To have me inside you, to be filled and pleasured until you can no longer walk? If you are mine, you will be mine in every way." His grip tightened on her shoulder as he spoke, his voice hot and passionate.

She ached at his words and released a shuddering breath. "Yes, if that's what you want."

His hand dropped as he took a step back. The ice returned, erecting a barrier between them.

Oh. He didn't want her. Disappointment swelled in her chest.

What other conclusion could she draw? He would marry her and go through the motions at the order of the king.

"Then you must understand my family," he said, producing a blue plastic straw from his pocket. He pinched the ends and the straw unrolled into a tablet. The screen glowed a soft blue.

"That's a good trick," she said.

He grunted, because he had a way with words. Writing with a stylus, he said, "This is my great-grandfather, King Edvar."

Sarah repeated the name, just in case there would be a test.

"By all accounts, a decent ruler. The kingdom prospered. His major failing was having too many children."

"You don't hear that criticism too often."

"Incorrect. Many noble families have been driven to ruin by dividing limited resources between too many offspring."

"So, grandpa couldn't keep it in his pants."

Vekele huffed, sounding amused. "Seven children. I will not bore you with the names. These three were given titles and lands in the core system. The remaining four are in the outer system. It was an adequate solution. The eldest child, Eglan, was the heir. Handsome, charming, and popular. He had been groomed to be the next king, and every account said he would be a good ruler."

"I'm sensing there's a twist in the story."

"He enjoyed microflyer racing," Vekele said. "He died in a crash. The official report declared the death accidental due to mechanical failure."

Sarah nodded, listening as Vekele rattled off the details in a cold, dispassionate fashion. This was old news to him, recounting the life and death of his grand uncle. Second uncle? Family trees were confusing.

"King Edvar had his suspicions but never openly accused one of his children of murdering their brother. As it happened, when the king died shortly after—"

"Under suspicious circumstances?"

"Under his third wife," he said in a dry tone.

Sarah pressed her lips together to keep from laughing. Vekele's lips twitched ever so slightly.

"The crown passed to Eglan's infant son. The remaining aunts and uncles acted as regents for the hatchling." He wrote down more names and drew lines connecting them. Sarah couldn't wait until she got an implant that allowed her to read. "The system worked well enough until the young king came of age and no longer listened to the regents. It went as well as you would expect."

"Not well at all?"

"The regents resented their loss of power. The council was ignored. The king made ill-advised decisions and implemented unpopular policies. When he died suddenly, no one was too upset."

"He just died?"

"Poisoned. The regents jostled for control and fought among themselves. My grandmother seized the throne. Yes, to answer the question you are burning to ask, she poisoned her nephew. It is a recurring theme in the family," he said, giving a casual wave of his hand. "She lasted twelve years as queen. My father ruled briefly. Both my parents were assassinated."

Sarah gasped in sympathy. "That's terrible."

He gave her a hard look. "It is politics. After that, the council could not agree on who should rule. Baris, a twelve-year-old child? Or appoint a regent? Or crown another from the outer worlds? Their claim to the throne was as strong as Baris'. Our uncle Serle locked us away here in Summerhall for our *safety*." He scoffed. "The details are not interesting."

Sarah perked with interest. Vekele had been imprisoned here? "I disagree. I think those details are very interesting. Did the house have the same security system? How long were you here? How long did the fighting last?"

"Did I wear a cuff on my ankle? Yes. Did I test the boundaries and have to be unchained, like a feral creature? Yes, many times. Did I kill my uncle for murdering my parents and locking me away?" A slow, vicious grin spread across his face.

"Yes," she said, answering his question.

"Yes," he repeated. "I was too young at first to wonder who ordered the assassination." He recalled that moment he emerged from the temple with Pitch, proud to have been selected by the karu for a bond, and found the blood, gore, and the remains of his parents. The devastating shock of it etched every detail into his mind. He said, "Baris quickly uncovered the conspirators."

"Your uncle?"

"That particular line has been extinguished. Only Serle's mate, Cassana, remains. I have no great love for that aunt, but Baris allows her to retain the title and property. When she eventually passes—either from traditional family murder or peaceful means—the title will go to a loyal cousin. The one thing my family does not lack is cousins."

"That's..." Cold. Vicious. Heartless. Adjectives kept popping into her mind. "Practical," she settled on.

The grin vanished, replaced again by the cold façade she knew so well. "That is the family you wish to tie yourself to. We murder one another for power and revenge. The peace Baris wants is fragile."

"You don't think it will last," she said.

He tucked her hair behind her ear, his thumb stroking her cheek. "I think it is fragile."

"How many cousins do you have out there who want their shot at the crown?"

"Too many."

In a moment of perfect clarity, she knew the story she was in.

She pressed her lips together to fight a grin. It wasn't even funny. It was terrifying. When that failed, she hid her inappropriate grin behind her hand. "I'm sorry. It's not funny. I'm not laughing. It's just all this time I've been thinking *Cinderella*, maybe *Beauty and the Beast*, but really it's *Game of Thrones*."

"This is serious, Sarah. Now is not the time for nonsense."

"I know, I know." Freaking *Game of Thrones*. Was this the first season where the only character she liked was executed? Or was everyone going to be eaten by dragons?

She took a breath and shook her hands, working out the need to giggle.

Serious. Be serious.

"I'm still doing it," she said.

"Sarah—"

"What are my options, Vekele? Get a job? I might not be able to go home and honestly—" She swallowed her next words, the ones that questioned if she even wanted to return home. She'd have to leave Ghost, and all she had waiting for her was an empty apartment and a long -ass commute to a job that barely paid the bills. She had her parents and the friends she never saw. That wasn't enough. She continued, "So, yeah, if the king is offering, I'm going to be a princess."

"You do not have to agree to this plan. You always have options," he said.

"Spoken like a man who's never been backed into a corner." Then, because she didn't know when to shut up, she said, "If it's not you, then it'll be some random cousin. Seems you've got a battalion of them."

He growled, sounding frustrated. The shadows darkened. Ghost's ears went back, issuing his own snarl.

"No," he said, his voice nearly a bark. "If you must take a mate, it will be me. I found you. *You are mine.*"

His chest heaved. His fists clenched. His eyes went inky black. Tension crackled in the air between them.

"Okay," she said, her voice soft and calm as she patted his chest.

He tilted his head at an extreme angle to look at her hand, still resting on his chest. His gaze was inhuman. It should have struck terror in her heart. Instead, the warmth of desire bloomed inside her.

"I want this. I want you. All those things you said. I want that," she said.

"To be my mate, in my bed, fucked until you can't remember your name and my seed spills out of you." His words were a challenge, even as they made her ache.

"Being crass won't scare me away, Prince Vekele," she said, stepping closer to him.

She knew him. He read to her the previous night until his voice went hoarse. He carried her to bed when she fell asleep in the library. He was thoughtful and, if not patient or polite, then good. He was a good man.

"There are things you should know about me," she said, since they were airing the dirty laundry. "I told you I was engaged to Robert."

"Your lost mate," he said, not sounding pleased. The black faded, and Vekele's expression returned to a guarded, neutral state.

"I love—loved—Robert with my whole heart. I told you about the brain aneurysm. I planned on spending my life with him and then one day he was gone." Her breath hitched in her throat. It was so strange explaining the man she had loved to the man she currently drooled over. She didn't feel as if she betrayed Rob by finding someone new. He'd want that. She worried that talking about Rob cheapened her feelings for Vekele, like it was a competition Vekele could never win.

It wasn't a competition. She had room enough in her heart to hold both. Rob would always be her past, but Vekele could be her future.

She smiled at him with watery eyes. He stepped to the side to better see her and tilted his head. All his hair flopped forward, covering his cloudy front eyes. His warm hand cradled the side of her face. Gently, he brushed away her tears.

Vekele wasn't a consolation prize. He was amazing.

"I was hurt and depressed and angry and sad," she said.

"That is a lot for one person to contain."

"I know. It was too much and everyone was so damn sympathetic and *nice* to me. It was gross. So I ran away. Metaphorically. Well, literally. I moved, got a new job, and hardly ever saw any of my old friends. I avoided anything that reminded me of… that reminded me. There was no color or life. It was just existing. That's no way to live." Her words spilled out in a jumble. There was a point to this rambling. There was. "So now I'm here and it's weird and scary, but also amazing. I feel like myself again. I know I'm going to carry this grief around with me for the rest of my life, and I'll always love Rob, but I'm not frozen anymore.

"And I like you. I said that before, but it's true. I like the way you pretend you're not super competitive when we play that game. I like it when you stay with me because I had a nightmare. I like you."

She paused, suddenly uncertain about Vekele's response. She barfed up her feelings and he looked properly horrified. "So, yeah. Since you shared your murder family with me, I thought you should know."

He watched her, saying nothing.

Typical.

"I won't apologize for having a life before you," she said. "You dragged out the literal skeletons from your family closet, and I'm cool with it. You can't pick your family."

"That is the moral lesson of my family history?" Amusement twisted through the bastard's voice.

"No, the lesson is that we've all got baggage. And I like you. I like you more than your murder family scares me." They should have scared her, the reasonable part of her brain told her, but gut instinct and self-preservation seemed to have the day off.

"Perhaps you are blinded by the opulence of royalty," he said.

"You chained me to a bed in a dusty room in a falling-down palace. That's not as enticing as you think it is."

His lips twitched. The jerk was enjoying her awkward confession of feelings.

"I found it enticing," he said, his voice a low purr. "I like you too, Sarah."

"Good," she said. Heat rose in her cheeks. Why was she blushing, and what should she do with her hands? Had they always been so weird and just there on the ends of her arms? She balled them into fists and stuck them behind her back.

"Good," he repeated. "But I will not take you as my mate because you think you have no other options."

Disappointment? Hello, again. Haven't seen you in a while.

Her eyes focused on the floor. It was easier to pretend she wasn't about to cry again if she didn't have to look at him.

"Be my mate because you want me," he said.

She lifted her gaze, only to find him watching her with a fierce intensity. "I do," she said.

He grinned in triumph, a blinding display of teeth and fangs against his dark gray lips. "Sarah Krasinski of Earth, you are my mate. When I found you, I knew you would change everything. I believe you were brought to this planet for me and me alone because I am that selfish and arrogant," he said. "Tell me you are mine."

That was the bossiest proposal she'd ever heard, but she loved every word of it. "I'm yours. I accept," she said.

His large hand wrapped about the back of her neck. He leaned down.

This was it. He was going to kiss her. Blubbering and tear-stained was not how Sarah pictured this moment.

Sarah closed her eyes and sighed, so ready for this.

His forehead pressed against hers. A rumbling, content noise came from deep in his throat.

Sarah opened her eyes. Vekele was right there, his eyes closed. Dark lashes rested against silvery gray skin.

It was intimate, perhaps more intimate than lips touching lips, because she was outside his field of vision. They were close enough that their breaths mingled. He was utterly vulnerable. Sarah couldn't imagine Vekele allowing himself to be vulnerable, yet there he was with the slightest hint of a smile on his face.

This wasn't the kiss she imagined, but this was nice, too.

CHAPTER TEN

SARAH

THEY IMMEDIATELY PREPARED TO LEAVE. Out of nowhere, a young-faced guard arrived. She recognized him from the temple. He had been with Vekele when the void beasts attacked her.

Vekele handed over her busted old phone. "Do not damage this, Luca."

"Fascinating. This generated the portal?" Luca turned the phone over in his hands.

"I'm not sure how, but I think so," Sarah said. "It's just my phone."

"Phone," Luca repeated, the word meaningless to him.

"We use it for communication, entertainment, taking pictures, and wasting time on games or apps." Embarrassment rose as she explained all the amazing things her extraordinarily powerful pocket-sized computer could do, that she only used to watch cat videos and listen to audiobooks.

"Oh, it is a tab. Would you like a replacement?" he asked.

"Yes, sure," she answered, glancing at Vekele in case that was not allowed. He seemed unconcerned.

"Set my mate up with a new unit when we arrive. She will require voice functionality until a translator chip is installed," Vekele said.

Luca nodded. "Will you instruct her on how to operate a tab, or shall I? I do not mind."

"Stop standing around. We need to return to the palace." Another guard entered the room. She was a tall woman, broad in the shoulders, and had long claws on her fingers. Her face was unfamiliar to Sarah, but she knew the voice. This woman had also been at the temple when Sarah fell through the portal.

"Kenth," Vekele said, his head dipping slightly in greeting.

"If you have finished flirting with the princess, get in the flyer," Kenth told Luca, whose face turned a shade darker.

"He wasn't flirting," Sarah protested.

"He was," Vekele said. "Is there anything you wish to bring?"

Sarah scanned the room. The clothes she wore when she came through the portal had been ruined. The busted phone was her only link to home.

"This," she said, grabbing the Karu and Beast game set. "And how was that flirting?"

"He could not take his eyes off of you. It was highly impertinent."

"Looking at me is rude?"

"Yes." His response was so matter-of-fact that it implied she misunderstood something fundamental about social behavior.

"You look at me all the time."

"That is different," he said, his voice stiff and formal.

Amusement bubbled up inside her. "Because you're a prince?"

"Because you are my mate." He brushed back a lock of her hair, tucking it behind an ear. His eyes went dark. "It pleases me to look at you."

Well, who could argue with that?

"I like looking at you too," she said.

THE CAPITAL CITY was a sprawling mass of gleaming towers, twisting and turning spires that defied logic.

Belts of greenery broke through the glass and steel. At first, it was a confusing jumble of buildings, roads, waterways, and green spaces. As the flyer circled the city, a pattern emerged.

The city sat at the juncture of two land masses, spread like wings. At the center was an island, completely dominated by a towering structure. Constructed of a light gray stone, azure tiles added a splash of color as they glistened in the sunlight. Tiered with too many arches and turrets to count, it sat at the convergence of three wide bridges, like a hawk in a nest. Considering the colors, it reminded Sarah of a blue jay.

The palace.

It was stunning and only a wee bit intimidating.

Vekele rested a hand on the back of her neck. It was a crudely possessive gesture, but the touch calmed her. She wasn't alone.

"You are ready," he said.

"I feel nauseous." She wasn't sure if it was her nerves, the flight, or Ghost, who curled miserably at her feet. He did not like flying.

"We will be on the ground soon."

The moment they landed, a flurry of attendants descended. They were to dine with the king and court in only three hours. Hardly any time at all to prepare. Stylists drew Sarah away to a private chamber to prepare her. Vekele went in the opposite direction with a cloud of attendants.

A woman with a scanner made a series of alarming noises as she took Sarah's measurements. Apparently, a tailored wardrobe would be waiting for her in the morning. Until then, Sarah had to make do with outfits the stylists brought.

It was so bizarre, having a team do her hair and makeup. Especially the makeup, as it was created for gray complexions with blue or lavender undertones. The makeup artist had no idea what to do with Sarah's beige skin. The result was horrific.

Her face had been painted white with blue circles of blush on her cheeks. Her hair had been piled high and powdered with charcoal that turned her fingers black when she accidentally touched her hair.

It was awful, but she could deal. Mainly, it felt bizarre having so many people speak to her at once. It had been just her and Vekele for so long. She enjoyed the quiet.

The owl tattoo on her arm received a dusting of a shimmering gold powder, so it wasn't all bad.

Then the unthinkable.

A stylist opened a case to display a crystal-studded dog collar.

"No. Absolutely not," she said.

"The beast—" The stylist held the collar out, letting the light catch in the crystal, like that would sway Sarah.

"I'm going to stop you right there," she said. "His name is Ghost. He is not a beast, and he is not a pet. I will not put a collar on him." They were still navigating their bond and what it meant, but she knew a collar was wrong. She'd worn a chain and would never do that to another being.

Ghost made the attendants nervous, but they honored her wishes and never mentioned the collar again. They dressed her in a sleeveless waistcoat over long, flowing skirts. The back laced up, allowing it to fit tightly. The lightweight fabric felt cool against her skin.

As the finishing touch, she was instructed to wear a set of silver talons. They fit over her fingers like rings with a delicate chain threading them together. Sarah flexed her fingers, certain she'd slice herself to ribbons.

"I don't think I can wear these," she said.

"Do not be silly. All females decorate their claws. It is unfortunate that yours are so short," the stylist said. Her claws—real claws—were covered in a sheath of intricate gold scrollwork.

"I'll cut myself or someone." She wiggled her fingers, trying to acclimate to the weight of them.

"Not that set. The tips are dull. To pierce the skin is intimate and—" The stylist flushed, a bluish tinge spreading over her face. "You would require a special-ized set for, umm, the prince's pleasure."

Laughter spread through the team, clearly knowing something that Sarah didn't. Still tittering and throwing around looks that said *things*, they packed up to leave. A new assistant coached Sarah on how to address the king, various nobility and titles, and proper dinner etiquette. She practiced using cutlery with the claws. Grasping a wine glass was too difficult. Exasper-ated after Sarah knocked over the third glass, she was advised to abstain from beverages.

Finally alone, Sarah examined her reflection. With the silver claws on her fingers, she tried and failed to pick up the skirt. Red flashed from hidden panels, which was a nice touch, but the black fabric combined with the heavy makeup washed out her complexion. She looked like a zombie.

With blue circles on her cheeks. A zombie clown.

A knock sounded on a door and Vekele entered. He was dressed in a similar style; only the color suited him.

"That is… interesting," Vekele said with caution. He wore a new jacket and waistcoat. The color was his typical black, but the fabric seemed crisp and rich. The lines hugged his form, drawing attention to his broad shoulders and the feather mantle. The feathers had a blue sheen. He also wore powder on his face, though it suited him. Kohl lined his eyes, making his eyes both more intense and broodier.

It was unfair how good he looked.

"I look like a clown." She poked at the blue circle on her cheek. The blunt end of the silver claw did not break the skin, as the stylist promised. "Or like the peasants are rebelling because I told them to eat cake. You, however, look good."

He plucked at the buttons on the coat. "It is adequate."

"Adequate, he says," she muttered, her tone playful.

Among the cosmetics left behind, Vekele grabbed a container of wipes. Carefully, he removed the heavy makeup. "Stay still. Do not squirm," he ordered.

"I don't squirm. Can you even see what you're doing?" Once the words left her mouth, she wished she could take them back. She sucked in a breath, waiting for a burst of anger or a scolding. "I'm sorry. I know you're sensitive… I mean, fuck. I'm sorry."

"I see you at this angle," he said, his tone calm, almost bored. "Do not treat me like an egg needing to be coddled. My sensibilities are not so fragile. I am blind in my front eyes."

"Well, for the record, your eyes look really hot like that. The eyeliner."

"Hot? Such a strange term for attractive."

She checked her reflection. Face freshly scrubbed; her skin had a pink glow. It was fine, right? The king expected a spectacle. Going au naturel would cause more of a stir than painting her face white like a doll. "Is this considered fashionable? The hair? The clown makeup?"

Vekele tilted his head, inspecting her. "It is court fashion. Most people do not dress in such a manner." He took her hand and inspected the ornamental claws. "However, these are worn by many."

"They mentioned a special set for your pleasure," she said, her voice falling to a whisper. She knew what that phrase meant and desperately wondered if it meant the same thing on Arcos.

Vekele had no visible reaction.

"Do not concern yourself," he said, releasing her hand with a gentle pat. "Let us do battle."

"I thought we were going to dinner."

"You did not mishear me."

VEKELE

Sarah's question about marking with her claws ran through his mind.

Her claws. Marking him. Claiming him.

He wanted the sharp, sweet sting of her claws on his skin. It was an old practice for females to mark their mates and often considered cruel, but his family remained unerringly traditional. It would be expected for Vekele to carry Sarah's mark. Her blunt human fingers were incapable of doing anything more than scratching. She would need a specialized set of ornamental claws, sharp enough to pierce his skin.

Pitch nipped at his ear, snagging his attention.

Just as well. It would not do to sit through the ordeal of a formal dinner while hard.

Dinner was held in the banquet room, a cavernous room that stretched for ages. As hatchlings, Baris and Vekele raced down the length on hovering boards. When the steward caught them, they were reprimanded for nearly damaging antique furniture and banished to the gardens.

Tonight, two long tables stretched the length of the banquet room. Baris sat at the head table, raised slightly on a platform. Chemical lingered from the fresh paint on the cream-colored walls. Gold shimmered on the wood trim. Crystal light fixtures. Deep red carpeting over stone floors.

The banquet hall was very different from the neglected room Vekele remembered. Money had been poured into renovating the banquet hall for the sole purpose of announcing that Baris had enough wealth and power to squander his fortune on elaborate meals and murals painted on the ceiling that no one would notice.

Visiting nobility and dignitaries, all invited to the palace for the treaty negotiations and the wedding, filled the space. Half the guests had their karu with them, perched on the back of specially designed chairs. Vekele recognized some faces. He had fought alongside some and clashed against others. One particular male glared at Vekele, obviously still upset about the ear that he lost to Vekele's blade.

Sarah's head swiveled back and forth, taking it all in. Ghost trotted at her side.

Alarm at the void beast rippled through the crowd, followed by whispers about Sarah's deformity.

"Is it tame? Will it attack us?"

"How dare they let that beast in here?"

"What happened to her?"

"The poor thing."

How dare they mock and pity his mate? His shoulder blades itched, his wings ready to unfurl in a massive display and remind them exactly who he was. Pitch echoed his sentiments.

Sarah's hand tightened on his arm. "Ignore them," she said.

They approached the head table. Baris sat at the center. His betrothed, Joie Starshade, sat to his right. Corde Starshade, her father, sat on the other side of the king. Councilor Raelle and other members of the Starshade family were also at the table.

Two empty seats waited for Sarah and himself.

Baris lounged in the chair, an arm dangling casually over its back. "What have you brought me, brother?"

The room fell quiet.

"I present Sarah Krasinski of Earth," Vekele said, his voice loud enough to carry through the hall. His words were overly formal, but they suited the situation. "I would ask the crown for permission to make her my mate."

The hall fell into stunned silence.

"Your mate? Explain." Baris leaned forward, intrigued.

Sarah stepped forward, Ghost right at her side. The void beast moved toward the king, tail wavering in a disturbing display as it moved in and out of shadows.

The guards at the wall tensed.

Sarah held out a hand, calling Ghost back. For a moment, the beast looked confused and very, very young. He recognized Baris and the karu and wanted to play.

"Not now. We talked about this, remember?" Sarah said in a placid tone. She rested a hand on Ghost's head. His tongue lolled out one side, a perfectly happy little beast.

The whispers started immediately.

"She tamed it!"

"I thought it was going to tear out the king's throat. I heard it growl."

Baris raised a hand to silence the hall. "Enough," he said, his voice rising above the din. He turned his attention to Sarah. "I do not recognize your name. What are you?"

"I'm human," she answered, projecting her voice to carry. "I was transported here accidentally. I landed at a place called Miria. Prince Vekele found me and has graciously allowed me to stay in his home these last two weeks."

Vekele glowed with pride at the way she commanded the crowd's attention. She delivered the practiced lines with natural ease, like a born performer. During the flight, they rehearsed the speech Vekele needed to deliver. It had not helped. Vekele was no actor. It was decided to let Sarah speak for herself.

"Since arriving, she has bonded with a void beast," Vekele said. "Which makes her of noble standing."

A murmur went through the crowd.

Ghost pressed against Sarah's legs. She reached down, touching his head to soothe him.

"Impressive. How did this happen?" Baris asked.

"It was unexpected, Your Majesty," she answered.

"And you intend to claim her as your mate?" He directed the question to Vekele.

"Yes."

"How did that happen?"

Vekele's brow furrowed, unsure how to answer. That was not part of the script.

"A male's reasons are his own, as is his heart," Baris said. He turned his attention back to Sarah now. "You bear the royal crest. Was that unintentional?"

She rubbed her arm with the mark. "It's based on an Earth animal, an owl. I've had it for a few years now."

Murmurs rolled through the crowd.

Councilor Raelle, an older female sitting a few seats away from Baris, leaned forward. "Your Majesty, this is most unusual, yet I cannot help but feel this is a sign from the fates."

Vekele disliked the councilor, largely because she kept to a rigid viewpoint that considered anything other than tradition to be spurious. She disliked change, and she was the principal opponent to the treaty with the Starshades.

A younger Vekele would have been surprised that such an elder would be so thirsty for battle. Now, he found the female aggravating.

"I concur," Baris said.

More whispers in the crowd. Very few believed in the fates. It was a superstitious concept that had fallen out of favor. However, the savvy in the audience—and the majority of those invited to the banquet were politically savvy—recognized how this alien female with a near -mythical bond and the royal crest could be a valuable political symbol.

The rest of the guests, the gossips—and Baris had made sure to invite the biggest gossips at court—would spread every gritty detail.

Sarah reached for his hand and squeezed. The gesture was unanticipated but comforting. He craved more touches. As much of her as she would allow.

And her claws marking his skin.

"Sarah Krasinski of Earth is a gift from fate, given to us in times of great change," Baris said.

Raelle looked pleased with herself. "Then you agree she must be bound to the royal house, honored as a mate of the king. To do less would be an insult."

An insult to whom?

Joie Starshade sat silently beside Baris. Her expression was blank, betraying no hint of her true thoughts, but fury burned in her eyes. The restraint she displayed was admirable. She'd make an excellent queen.

Corde Starshade had no such restraint. He stood, knocking his chair back from the table. "We came to negotiate peace. If you will throw away the treaty on this... novelty, we will have no part of this farce."

"Please, calm yourself. I fully intend to settle the terms of the treaty and bind my hand to Joie. There is another in the Shadowmark house who wants to properly honor this gift," Baris said. "The fates brought Sarah Krasinski of Earth to Miria, for Prince Vekele. He felt the call to journey to Miria and discovered her there."

"Rescued me," Sarah added. "For the record. I was attacked by a pack of void beasts."

"Your Majesty, you cannot ignore the fates," Raelle said.

Baris held up a hand to silence the councilor. "I agree. I cannot ignore the fates. Vekele, brother, shall you honor this gift and treasure her as your mate?"

"I shall," he said, his throat suddenly dry.

"I grant you permission to claim this female as your mate and wish you both much joy."

The crowd burst into noise, everyone having an opinion and needing to share it with their nearest neighbors.

"The marriage should be done at once, even if other events," Raelle said, casting a glance at the Starshades, "have to be delayed."

Baris grinned; it was slow and a touch vicious. "What an excellent suggestion, Raelle. But I see no reason to delay. Remind me, your position allows you to officiate weddings, yes?"

"Yes," Raelle answered, hesitation in her voice. "But a royal wedding requires planning and a certificate. You cannot just tie a ribbon on two people and call it legal."

Vekele pulled a length of red ribbon and a folded paper from his inner coat pocket. He handed them to Baris. "I think this will do."

Baris unfolded the marriage certificate with dramatic flair. "Excellent. Let us bind these two souls together."

SARAH

Vekele held out a hand, palm up. Sarah placed her hand in his.

The officiant wrapped the ribbon around the hands, binding them together. Sarah barely registered the words as she repeated them. Vekele watched her with such intensity that it made her squirm, as though he could see through the layers of clothing and makeup, stripping her bare. Naked.

Married. Sarah volunteered for this. In the garden that morning, it seemed abstract. A notion. They told her what to expect, but now that it was happening, it felt unreal.

The officiant stopped speaking. People clapped politely.

A wicked grin spread across Vekele's face, white fang against dark gray lips. He pulled on the ribbon, tugging her forward. She stumbled forward into his arms.

"You are mine," he whispered in her ear. His voice sent a flutter of anticipation through her entire body.

Sarah understood. That look was desire, raw and unchecked.

CHAPTER ELEVEN

VEKELE

THE SECURITY SCANNER read his thumbprint, and the doors to his quarters opened.

"You know, it's a tradition on Earth for the groom to carry the bride over the threshold of their home," she said.

"To further Arcos-Earth relations, I will honor this tradition." He scooped her up into his arms, cradling her against his chest. She gave a startled laugh and relaxed in his hold.

Once inside, she gasped. "All this is yours? It's so fancy."

"It is a basic set of rooms." He seldom stayed at the palace and cared little for the decor. The rooms were styled in the standard opulent fashion, no different from any other suite.

Reluctantly, he set her down on her feet. "What other Earth traditions should we observe?"

"Well, there's the wedding night." Pink flushed in her cheeks. Such a delightfully odd color.

"I suspect we share the same tradition." Heat flooded his voice. "I cannot wait to taste you, my mate."

The pink blush intensified. "Yeah, same. Hard same," she said.

Before they could enjoy their wedding night, there were a few practical matters to handle. He added Sarah to the palace's security system. Her thumb print and eye scan would allow her access to the computer network, entertainment system, and comm network, and open nearly every door.

Pitch and Ghost settled down for the night in the sitting room. The pup whined at not being allowed in the bedroom, as he normally was, but eventually climbed onto the massive, cushioned sleeping pad. The void beast's bed looked more luxurious than most beds Vekele had slept in.

With that task finished, he led his mate into the bedchamber.

Sarah stood in the center of the room, in the center of a puddle of moonlight. Her free arm wrapped over her stomach in a defensive gesture. It pained him to see his mate so uneasy.

"You have no reason to be nervous," he said. "I have seen you naked and find your form pleasing."

She closed her eyes and gave a slow shake. "Honestly, Vekele, I don't know how you manage to be sweet and rude at the same time."

"Innate talent." No one had ever accused him of being sweet before. Rude, yes. Often. But never sweet. He liked it.

"Ah, that must be it," she said, amusement in her voice. Her shoulders relaxed, and her hands fell away from the guarded position. Somehow, his words put her at ease.

The red ribbon tied them together. He did not wish to remove it yet.

"So, we're married," she said.

"Yes."

"That was legally binding?"

"In three days, we will sign a certificate, but that is a formality, mainly for the media. This," he said, giving the ribbon a gentle tug, "is done."

"Media? You mean a press conference with questions?"

"Yes. The press office will provide a list of acceptable questions to the press and give us the acceptable answers."

She chewed on her bottom lip. "Why not just issue a press release?"

"People will want to see their lovely princess."

She huffed in amusement. He adored the sound. "I doubt that."

Truthfully, he did not want to share his mate with the media or anyone. She was for him and him alone.

"Can I ask you something?" Her voice sounded unsure. He disliked her lack of confidence. His princess should never doubt herself or her importance to him.

"Ask."

"Can we be honest with each other? Whatever happens —in bed, in public—we're honest. I don't want lies or misunderstandings."

"I have always been honest with you and will continue to do so." It was an easy promise to make. "Now let me admire my princess," he said.

Vekele circled her as much as the ribbon allowed, admiring her from all sides. She did not wear the typical court gown, although she had looked attractive with the fitted waistcoats and high collars. This gown had no such collar. It looked unfinished; the bodice plunged to expose the swell of her breasts. Her arms were bare, exposing the royal mark inked into her skin, although bare arms were the fashion for the summer heat. The black silk suited her. The hidden red panels in the skirt that flashed as she moved suited her even better.

He could not wait to see how the gown looked discarded on the floor.

The moonlight cast a soft glow on her hair. Stray wisps framed her face, a quickfire color that shifted and vanished in the light. Hair pins studded with crystals sparkled.

"What?" she asked.

"I want to remember this moment," he said, standing at her side. He reached for a pin, releasing a lock of hair. Heavily powdered in the current style, the gray failed to mask the red. One by one, the pins came out and dusted red locks tumbled down her back.

She was too lovely to bear.

His hand rested on the back of her neck, and he dipped his head down to hers.

Their foreheads pressed together. He listened to her breathing, quick and nervous. Her body was tense. It was entirely unacceptable.

"This is a gesture of affection," he said.

"Oh," she said, sounding surprised. Then, "You've done this before. After Ghost arrived."

"I was frightened. I was relieved that you were unharmed," he said.

In the past, he had been loath to mention any point of weakness or fear. Those sentiments could be used against him. With Sarah, it was easy. She would not turn his emotions against him, except to lightly tease him when he deserved it. Never as a weapon. Never to hurt.

"Is this like a hug? Because I enjoy hugs. Very pro -hug here."

He wrapped his free arm around her. The bound arm stayed at their side. "It is like an embrace, but more intimate. It is for loved ones." To stand so close to another person was to be vulnerable. Vekele could not remember the last time he had embraced anyone in this manner. Probably his brother, years ago.

"I like it," she said, her voice soft.

"May I touch you?" he asked.

She twisted her head to look at him. "Yes, but can we talk about sex for a minute?"

"You have questions," he said, unable to resist the urge to tease his mate. "What happens between mates can be many things, but it should always be pleasurable for both people. Or all, but that is not what I prefer. I don't intend to share."

"All? Oh my word, Vekele, you're killing me." Her face flushed a bright pink, but she laughed. "I know what sex is. I want to know how it will work between us, because," she stumbled, "because I can't stop thinking about what you said earlier today."

He leaned, his lips brushing against the shell of her round ear. "Remind me."

"You know…"

"Is my mate shy? I am shocked." His fingers traced a path down her throat.

"You know I'm not."

"Then tell me."

"To share a bed."

Desire rumbled deep in his throat. He slipped a finger under the dress' strap, letting it slide over her beige skin.

"I can't think when you do that," she said.

"What else?"

"I'm not… I'm not good at dirty talk." The pink flush returned to her skin.

"I disagree. You have my full attention." He gently tugged the ribbon binding them together, pulling her back until she pressed against his front. At this angle, she was nothing but a blur of powdered hair and pale skin. His hands skimmed over her shoulders, trailing down her arms, partly to explore her features but also to reassure himself of her location.

Her back arched, leaning into his touch. He nuzzled the curve of her neck, then licked the flesh. A clean burst of soap and salt blossomed on his tongue.

"Can we slow down for a minute?" she asked.

Vekele stepped back as far as their joined hands allowed. "Are you uncomfortable? Do you not want this?"

She turned to face him. "I do. I want this. I want you."

Satisfaction rolled through him at her words. She wanted him.

"But this is happening so fast."

"You have been sleeping in my bed for weeks," he said.

"But you've been all…" she said, waggling her fingers in his direction.

"I do not know what that means."

"Cold. Aloof with your sneering prince face."

"That is my face. You like my face."

"Resting prince face. Right." She sighed, then a smile tugged on her lips. She reached for him, playing with the buttons on his shirt but not undoing them.

Frustrating.

"Are we even compatible?"

"Very. Do you think anyone else would dare be so insolent to me? Or demanding? Or find me amusing? You are mine, Sarah Krasinski. How often must I tell you this?"

"More than you're doing now, apparently."

"Then I will tell you every day." He pressed his forehead to hers, closing his eyes and breathing in her scent. Underneath the powder and perfume that tickled his nose, he found her scent. It was rain and summer heat, fresh earth, and an overgrown garden. "I will show you."

"I mean, do the bits and pieces work together?"

"Conception may require the assistance of a medic. According to the reports on humans, Khargals have bred with humans without medical intervention. Arcosians can breed with Khargals, so I do not anticipate encountering difficulties when we breed."

"Wow, breeding. You just jumped right to that."

"That is a consequence of fucking," he said, pushing back another unruly strand of hair behind her round ear. "Make no mistake, I *am* going to fuck you. Hard. Gently. Repeatedly. Every way we can imagine. I do not think I will tire of it."

She licked her lips. "Sounds like we might die of exhaustion."

"An acceptable risk."

He hooked a finger under the other strap and slid it down. Sarah clutched the front of the gown to her chest.

"I'll show you mine if you show me yours," she said in a playful tone.

Vekele took her hands in his, removing them from the gown. One strap caught on her wrist, unable to fall away with their joined hands. He growled, snapping the fragile strap. The fabric fell to the floor with a whisper.

She was stunning.

He would never tire of this sight. His gaze swept over her, taking in her curves at a leisurely pace. Moonlight caught the golden cosmetic powder, making her glow like a celestial being. She was his to worship, and he fully intended to express his devotion at her altar.

"Well, am I so different?" she asked, her voice sounding nervous.

"Smaller. Rounder. Pinker. Are they supposed to be that color?" His fingers twitched, wanting to touch her nipples. They were the color of crushed berries.

She glanced down. "Oh, yeah, that's my normal color. What about you?" She reached for him and unbuttoned his shirt. "Lavender? Lilac?"

She pushed down his shirt, the fabric bunching at his elbow. Again, their bound hands prevented the shirt from being removed.

That could be a problem. He wanted the full range of motion with his mate, not to be restricted by clothing.

Sarah seemed to sense his thoughts. "We can untie our hands."

"Not yet," he said. "The ribbon stays until we consummate our union."

"We'll deal."

He might tear the shirt to shreds, but yes. They would *deal*.

"May I?" she asked.

He nodded.

She stepped out of his field of vision, directly in front of him, and placed her hand on his chest. She leaned in; his breath warm against his skin. Her tongue, wet and hot, brushed against him.

He jolted.

"Sorry, I should have warned you," she said.

"Do it again," he ordered.

She complied, teasing and sucking his nipple. His hand rested on the back of her head.

He wanted to see what she looked like with her lips on his nipples. He wanted to see every flutter of her lashes, every half-smile as if she knew a secret, and feel every sigh. For the first time, he felt true anger at the person who bungled his assassination attempt. They took this from him.

His fingers wove through her hair.

She pulled away. Still in his blind spot, she fumbled with the front of his trousers. "What do you have in here?"

"The usual two cocks."

SARAH

Two.

She gulped. "Well, I just got the one vagina."

"Only one?" He sounded intrigued.

"How many are you expecting?"

He grinned. "One. Do not be alarmed."

Easy for Mr. Two Dicks to say. "Well, now I've got to know." She opened the front of his trousers and pushed them down. Hard, his cocks sprang free.

Yup. Two.

Stacked on top of each other, they looked intimidating. Dark gray, flushed purple at the ends, and ridged.

"Can I?" she asked, reaching out her hand.

"Touch me any way you like."

He stood still as she stroked the top dick. It tapered to a point. Ridges ran along the top and bottom. She could easily picture how the top and bottom ridges locked together.

She stroked his length, wondering at the feel of the ridges.

Glancing up, he bit his lower lip in concentration.

"Is this good?"

"Yes."

She gave him a few more strokes, then said, "I want to use my mouth."

He gasped. "Do it."

She kneeled on the plush carpet and nuzzled the crease where his groin met his hip. He smelled good of clean soap and musk.

She licked the base of the top cock, running her tongue along the ridges. Her other hand grasped his lower cock, holding it at the base. As she licked his length, she pumped her hand on the other. The tip leaked, and she smeared precum along his shaft.

Taking him as deep as she could, she wondered if she would ever be able to take both at once. Her jaw ached at the idea, but her core throbbed with the want of it.

His hips rocked forward. She relaxed her jaw, letting him move in and out of her mouth. Hands rested lightly on the top of her head. He murmured soft words of praise.

Finally, he pulled away. "On your back. I will taste you."

She scrambled to the bed; the red ribbon pulled taut as he crawled in after her.

His blue eyes burned, catching the dim light in the room, and shining.

She spread her legs, opening herself to him.

His hands gripped her knees, holding her open. He stared at her pussy intently, like he was studying for a test. A groan rumbled in his chest. "You are lovely."

"Not weird?"

"Do you find me weird?"

Sarah was tempted to make a joke or say he was a little weird but decided against it. They vowed to be honest with one another. "No," she said. "You're different than I expected, but I like it. I like you."

He murmured some reply, too low to hear. His fingers brushed against the curls between her thighs.

"And I find you intriguing. What is this?" His thumb stroked her clit.

Her hips jolted off the bed. "My clit," she cried.

"Is it pleasurable?"

"Very, just sensitive. Touch it softly."

Another murmured response. This time, his fingers stroked her folds, circling her clit. She moaned at the sensation. Pleasure coiled in her, winding tight and not letting go.

He lowered his head, licking her sensitive flesh. He paid particular interest to her clit, as if fascinated by the noises his touch drew from her. The man was a wizard with his tongue, dipping into her core, and sucking on her clit.

He watched her, his cloudy front eyes blank, but the blue ones tracking her every response.

She grabbed the hand he had placed on her knee, teasing at the ribbon tying them together. Her free hand went to his hair, twisting and tugging.

It was too much, too intense, and too fast. Her climax grew and grew, filling her, driving out her breath. She cried out, jerking her hips away to break contact.

He followed, settling between her thighs. "Are you ready for me?"

Yes. She wanted him in her. Now. "I want to try. Just one?"

"One at a time." He lined himself up and pushed in.

Her core burned as he stretched her, filling her inch by delicious inch. It had been so long since anything felt pleasurable. She knew she'd come quickly.

And often.

He planted a hand next to her shoulder, the ribbon pulling her arm at an awkward angle. She wrapped her legs around his waist. His weight went forward, adding extra force as his hips drove forward.

It was too good.

"Yes, Vekele, yes. Like that."

Her hips lifted, letting him in deeper still. Their bodies moved, rising and falling in uncoordinated movement. It was awkward but felt too good to stop.

Then perfection. They moved together, push, and pull working in harmony, skin on skin meeting with delicious friction. He was gorgeous, his eyes always on her, watching. Nothing went unnoticed. Every touch was important. Every moan to be savored. She felt cherished. Not a burden or duty given to him by the king but wanted. Desired.

Sensation built inside her, swelling to the point it would consume her. She clutched at his back, digging her fingernails in.

His eyes went dark, inky dark shadows gathering. Need exploded in her, responding to the urgency in his touch. Every nerve ending sang. It was too much and not enough. Ecstasy broke over her as she called his name.

"My mate," he growled, teeth clenched. His entire body tensed as he sighed and emptied himself inside her.

Before she could wonder if they were finished, he withdrew, and his second cock pushed its way in. He fell forward, her feet now over his shoulders. His thrusts were erratic, pumping into her hard.

Desire ignited in her again. They moved as one. Her prince, always so reserved and careful with his words, could not keep himself quiet. He said she was beautiful. He loved the way she felt when she was full of his seed. So good. So tight. She was his. Only his.

She responded in kind, loving the way he felt inside her. Used her. Needed her.

It couldn't last. Pleasure peaked again; her throat shouted raw as she cried out. He licked her neck, where the curve met the shoulder, and bit.

For a moment, the sting of the bite did not register. Bliss kept her floating and fuzzy. He thrust, his hips snapping, and groaned, his face nuzzled against her neck.

He licked the bite, then rolled to the side, pulling her with him.

"Did you bite me?"

"Instinct," he said. "I should have warned you. Does it hurt?"

She lifted her hand to check, dragging his bound hand with it. Huffing in frustration, she touched the area with her free hand. "Oddly, no."

"A male's saliva neutralizes the pain."

"Oh. Good to know." Then, "Is that something you want from me? To bite you?"

He rose to one elbow and regarded her. "No. Female Arcosians mark their mates with their claws."

"I don't think I'll be able to do that."

"You scratched my back. Is it a fierce mark?" He sat up, allowing her to see his back and the red welts she left.

She touched the marks. "They're just scratches. They'll go away in a few hours."

"A shame. I would like everyone to know how I satisfied my mate." He lay back down and pulled her to him.

She rested her head on his chest. His heartbeat was a steady rhythm, lulling her to sleep.

"Can we untie the ribbon?" she asked, yawning.

"Not just yet," he said.

They stayed like that, nestled up to each other until dawn.

CHAPTER TWELVE

SARAH

LATE MORNING LIGHT crept across the carpet. The air warmed. The bedsheet drifted away, exposing her legs. Vekele's arm resting over her waist kept the sheet from slipping to the floor. Sleep had been elusive, partly due to the new bed but mostly due to the person next to her.

Vekele was fire or ice. No middle ground. Once he removed the mask of the cold, aloof prince, he was a man of burning passion. They spent the night exploring, teasing, and tasting, and finally fell into something resembling sleep just as the sky turned pearly gray with the promise of dawn.

"So you are not a dream after all," he murmured, burying his face in the tangle of his mate's hair. His hard—how?— cocks ground against her bottom.

"There is no way you're ready again," she said. "What kind of vascular system do you have to support two dicks that are hard all the time?"

He chuckled, his voice right at her ear. "A superior vascular system, obviously, but this is only for you."

Sarah sighed, her core aching at his deep laugh. No one had a right to have such a sexy laugh. She rolled over to face him.

"Is this okay?" she asked.

He pressed his forehead to hers. "Better than okay."

"Tolerable?"

Another chuckle. Another fluttering ache. She was sore, and parts of her twinged from being used for the first time in years, but damned if her body wasn't on board for another round. Had she always been this lascivious? She hadn't felt desire for anything—person or vibrator— in so long she'd forgotten what having a libido was like. Or maybe this was a hormonal change now that she was in her thirties.

Don't look a gift horse in the mouth.

Right, right.

"Perfection," he said.

Sarah kissed him, cautious of morning breath. He groaned, deepening the kiss.

"This is for me?" She reached down, taking both cocks in hand. They were a… handful. Fine, that was bad. She was too turned on to care, ready to stuff herself with a double helping of princely penis.

He pumped his hips, fucking himself in her fist. "Only for you," he said.

Then Vekele had to ruin her perfectly lecherous moment by being romantic.

"How are you so sweet? Like, no one knows you're a total cinnamon roll."

He stilled. "Are you hungry? Is that why you compare me to a pastry?" He pulled away. "We will eat. I have been selfish and neglected you. I will bring you water."

"No, you don't. I'm not done with you." Sarah grabbed his hand and pulled him back to bed. "You are going to finish what you started, mister."

And he did.

Twice.

THE FIRST DAY, they kept the world at bay, too wrapped up in each to care for anyone else.

The following morning, the world would not wait. Outfits had to be fitted. Stylists came to do her hair. Again. It was a whole Cinderella experience. Public relations managers had a list of questions and acceptable answers to be memorized. A medic installed a translator chip into her head and a dose of pain meds for the headache from said chip being implanted in her brain.

A particularly stern-faced man arrived to coach Sarah in court etiquette. How to walk. How to talk. How to stand perfectly still like a statue, because that was what people did at court, apparently: standing around looking beautiful but not actually doing anything. The mice in the story never yelled at Cinderella because her poor posture was common and insulting.

After hours of frustration, the instructor pronounced her a barbarian but passable for polite company. Hooray.

Sarah got why Vekele ran away from palace life to his house in the mountains.

The palace was, well, a palace. She hadn't been given a tour, but what she saw was stunning and more advanced tech-wise than she expected. Summerhall had electricity and hot water, but that wasn't so different from her apartment back on Earth. Just fancier with gilding and a lot more rooms.

The palace had an AI to answer questions, play music, light a path along the floor to guide Sarah through the labyrinth of the palace, and it even gave her the weather report.

Screens that were nothing more than a thin layer of glass that floated. Just floated. Sometimes they floated over a console table. Sometimes it was against a wall like a flat -screen TV. The screen had amazing clarity and if Sarah left a room with a program playing, the program followed her from screen to screen.

The biggest surprise was Arcosian soap operas. She asked the AI to randomly play a program, curious to see what alien pop culture looked like. What she got was a long -running series—think decades—of half-hour programming with dramatic stares into the camera and lovers clutching each other passionately.

She had no idea what was happening. There was a dude—a doctor, maybe? —in the military. He left behind his sweetheart to fight for the king. When he returned home, his brother had stolen his inheritance and his sweetheart. So the dude did the logical thing of marrying literally the first woman he saw, a disheveled maid. The cast acted as if the maid were hideous, but no amount of dirt and bad makeup could hide the way the actress glowed.

It was amazing. Sarah was hooked.

Vekele found her curled up on the sofa, her eyes glued to the screen on the far wall. "I refuse to believe you enjoy this."

"Don't judge. This is fascinating." She was certain she missed nuance and cultural references. No one said anything directly, or maybe they did with body language, and she didn't understand.

He watched for a moment, then made a dismissive noise. "We have books. An entire library. A library bigger than Summerhall."

"That's your judgy tone."

They proceeded to watch another two episodes, where Vekele told her all the ways the characters made bad decisions, the program was not historically accurate—she had no idea it was a historical drama—and the main character was always diving into the ocean with his clothes on.

It was like Vekele didn't understand the nature of gratuitous scenes with that handsome actor in wet clothes, emerging dramatically from the ocean, having rescued a kitten or whatever needed to be rescued that episode. She wasn't even from the same planet and she got it.

News programs were entirely different. Sarah had no idea who or what the newscasters spoke about on the programs. She understood the words, obviously, but she didn't know any of the names or places.

Something happened to someone. It was bad.

Another thing happened to a different person. It was good.

Occasionally, the programs played footage of Vekele and Sarah at the banquet. She couldn't watch. The cringe factor was too high.

Finally, on the third day, she and Vekele would sign the certificates and speak to the press.

No big. Just the eyes of a multi-planetary kingdom will be on you.

The stylist—she still wasn't over having a stylist—dressed her in a snug teal waistcoat with a waterfall cut over slim black trousers. Sleeveless, of course, to display her owl tattoo. Fabric flowed over her hips, moving with every step. The collar stood up but was nothing like the elaborate collars on the clothes Vekele found for her at Summerhall. Makeup was kept simple, with no gray paint or powder. The shoes were even comfortable.

As the stylist debated a lip color, an older woman entered the apartment. The woman wore her hair piled high and powdered so thoroughly that a dusty cloud drifted in her wake. She wore a stiff collar that came nearly to the tops of her pointed ears. The golden caps on her claws appeared soft, as if made from silicone. Delicate chains stretched from the caps to a thick bracelet on either wrist.

Quality shone through in her ensemble, but Sarah couldn't say if it was fashionable, good taste, or overly formal. The soap opera didn't cover court fashion.

"You may leave," the woman said, dismissing the stylist.

"Excuse me," Sarah said. "Who are you?"

The woman ignored her. Instead, she circled Sarah, examining her with a critical gaze. From the distaste on her face, she didn't like what she saw.

"You are smaller than I expected; not minuscule, more like you were stretched too tall. No substance to your bones," the woman said at last.

"I'm perfectly average for a human," Sarah said. The woman stood a head taller than her. Everyone she met on the planet seemed to be taller than her, so maybe she was pint-sized.

"Going without makeup is a wise choice. Play up to that primitive look."

Primitive?

"I'm sorry. Who are you again?"

"The king's aunt, here to ensure that you do not embarrass the royal family in front of the media."

"From what I've heard, Baris and Vekele have a dozen aunts and uncles. Which one are you?" Sarah stepped back from the woman, putting distance between them.

An assassin would have to have balls of steel to march into a room, dismiss the staff, and pretend to be family, but better to be cautious and alive than bleeding out on the floor. That lesson she learned from watching *Game of Thrones*.

Ghost came to her side, his body tense and his tail puffed.

"I am Lady Cassana." She gave a weak laugh. "And if I wanted you dead, you would be dead."

"That sounds like the family motto."

Cassana was not amused.

Ghost growled, pressing close to Sarah's legs.

The woman's gaze snapped down to Ghost. "So the reports were true. You bonded with a beast. The primitive woman and her monster."

Instinctively, Sarah placed a hand on Ghost's ruff. It centered her as much as it calmed him.

"I should not be surprised," Cassana continued. "Vekele was always dragging home wild things he thought he could tame."

"If you came here to insult me, you can leave." Sarah struggled to keep her voice even and betray the panic rising in her stomach. No puking before the press conference. That was definitely on the list of no-nos the assistant gave her.

"I came here to prevent you from embarrassing the family," Cassana said. "That color is abhorrent. Stand still." She grabbed a cloth off the dressing table and scrubbed Sarah's mouth with more force than necessary.

Sarah flinched away from the claws. Capped or not, she didn't trust them not to be razor sharp. The chains tinkled as Cassana worked to apply a more suitable lip color. This close, Sarah noticed the bracelet. It was very familiar. In fact, it was exactly like the security cuff Vekele had placed on her ankle.

Cassana caught Sarah staring. "Ah, you see my jewelry; a one-of-a-kind piece, given to me by the king after the death of my mate."

"You're a prisoner."

She gave an icy smile and her eyes remained empty. "Spared as a grand gesture of the King's benevolence but confined here. It could be much worse. Who else has such a luxurious prison?"

"A cage is a cage, even in a palace," Sarah said, mentally scanning through what Vekele had shared of his family's history. This was the wife of the uncle who had been executed, the last of that branch. That uncle had also assassinated Vekele's parents, so it was not an unjustified execution.

Fuck. This family was nothing but murder, imprisonment, and treachery. She wouldn't be surprised if some younger sibling had walled up an heir in the cellar. That seemed on brand.

Cassana stepped back to consider the lip color. "You are nothing like they say."

"What do they say?" Sarah asked, despite knowing she shouldn't play this woman's game.

"That you are a fierce warrior. You tamed a beast." Cassana's icy smile returned. "And that you even tamed a void beast."

"Are you implying that Vekele is the beast?" Offense wormed its way into her. She didn't enjoy Cassana's not-so-subtle jabs, but she ignored them. Vekele, however, was off limits, which was absurd. He'd be the first to tell her that he didn't need his feelings protected.

Cassana's eyes gleamed. Why couldn't Sarah keep her mouth shut?

"While the gossipmongers consider you worth gossiping about, you are quite valuable beyond that. Baris was right to lock you away with Vekele. Better to have you as his captive than to let you be a rival's pawn. You see, we are both prisoners in this very fine cage. You can hardly notice the bars." She waved a distracted hand to the well-appointed room.

Turning her attention back to Sarah, she frowned. "Pink is such an unusual color, but it suits you. Now, remember to smile. If you are asked a question not on the list or you cannot remember an approved answer, say, 'I am honored to be here.' Easy, yes?"

"Sure. Easy," Sarah said, mind already spinning. Cassana had said nothing that Baris didn't already say, albeit in a more cynical take. Sarah knew her choices had been to marry Vekele or some random member of the family that supported Baris. She *knew* that. Yet Cassana's word shook her.

She shouldn't have let the woman play games with her, but the damage had been done.

VEKELE

Something happened to Sarah. When he arrived, she had been dressed and groomed to the court's impeccable standards. The garment accentuated every appealing aspect of her form. He was an uninteresting lump in a stuffy costume compared to her glory. The media would adore her.

Yet her lips were pressed together in that way she had that indicated she was upset.

"Tell me," he ordered.

"There's nothing to tell. I hope I don't regret these shoes." She bent over to adjust a strap.

Vekele touched her arm, causing her to stand up straight. "Tell me what makes you upset."

"It's silly. Your aunt Cassana paid me a visit. I know she wanted to rattle my cage," she said, color draining at the words, "but she still got to me."

"That one will drip poison in your ear if you let her," he said. "Do not let her upset you."

"Well, lesson learned. Is it time?"

"Yes." He held out an arm for her. She hooked their arms together, and they made their way to the ceremony.

"Was she involved in your parents' murder?" Sarah asked, her voice barely a whisper.

"Undoubtedly. She was complicit in keeping Baris and me captive at Summerhall. No matter what she tells you, she is not innocent. My uncle was executed for high treason."

"But she was spared."

"Baris believes it is better to hold a viper in your hand than let it slither away."

Sarah shivered at his words. "I can't believe I'm saying this, but maybe just chop off the viper heads? A handful of vipers cannot be good for your health."

"When we have completed our obligations, we will leave the palace."

"For Summerhall?"

Vekele did not know how to interpret that look on her face. "If you wish, but I am a wealthy male with several properties, some on Arcos and some off-planet." He had never felt the need to visit his estates; whether they were located in the inner core planets of the kingdom or the far reaches, their draw was negligible. "We will tour them all, then you can make your decision."

She rewarded his clever notion with a warm smile. "I'd like to travel and see your corner of the universe, not just the bits you own." Hastily, she added, "Though I'm sure you own the most interesting bits."

"I have never been bothered to visit any of them. The military kept me busy." Now he had nothing but time on his hands, yet it did not feel like a punishment. It felt like an opportunity. Mainly he liked the way his mate asked to see more of his world, rather than be returned to hers. He vowed to keep her too distracted to think of Earth.

The ceremony to sign the marriage certificate was arranged in one of the many receiving rooms. Walls that normally partitioned off the space had been folded back, opening up the room. A table draped in an excessively expensive cloth was raised on a small platform at one end. The media were contained at the far end, some attending in person and others via avatar on screens. Open balcony doors allowed in the afternoon breeze.

High-ranking members of the court and nobility sat near the signing table. Vekele recognized a cousin or two. Karu perched in the rafters above or on the balcony. He did not see anyone in attendance from the Starshades. Interesting.

Baris stood behind the table next to the royal clerk. His betrothed was absent. Discreetly, almost cloaked in shadow, the royal guards waited in the background.

"This is certainly more attention than I have ever earned myself," Vekele said, speaking quietly enough for only Sarah to hear.

"More than I've ever had, too."

"Do not be nervous. No matter what happens, everyone must clap politely and declare the ceremony a triumph, or they will be executed."

His words echoed in the suddenly quiet room, louder than he anticipated.

Sarah's laughter filled the awkward silence. She lightly hit his arm in that playful way of hers. "Your jokes are the worst. Timing is everything."

Polite laughter rippled through the crowd. The tension in his shoulders relaxed. However clumsy and graceless he was at court; his mate was princess material.

The ceremony itself was simple. A court clerk read the certificate of marriage. Vekele signed his name and many, many titles.

Sarah signed her infinitely more efficient name.

Pleasure filled him. They had been bound by oath and ribbon. Now they were bound by ink.

They posed by the signed certificate for the media feed. Questions came rapid-fire from the crowd.

"Human princess, how do you find marriage?"

"What do you think of Arcos?"

"Do all humans look like you?"

Sarah's smile never wavered, despite the strain in her eyes. She kept her answers short and within the prescribed list of acceptable responses. In short, she was perfect.

"What do you like best about Prince Vekele?" The question came from the back.

"I like his laugh," she said without hesitation.

A brief, stunned silence fell over the crowd. Then a titter rippled through the room. The media adored her.

Questions swung to Vekele. He had never been anything other than the grim-faced soldier to them, but now they asked too many questions about his opinions on useless items, like sports. Honestly. He had no opinion on the league or whatever championship was currently being held.

Then the tone of the questions changed, shifting from the simple questions about his new mate to ones with a harder edge.

"How do you feel about the king's efforts for peace?"

"Does the treaty erase your military victories?"

"Why was the investigation on your attack closed so quickly, Prince Vekele?"

"Do you plan retaliation against those responsible for your attack?"

"Rumor has it that you believe the king ordered the attempt on your life?"

The last question rang through the suddenly silent crowd.

Anger welled up inside him, and the shadows gathered to him. Pitch dug her claws into his shoulder, agitation coming through their bond.

How dare...

Sarah touched his hand, focusing his thoughts. He would retain his composure. A few rude questions would not ruin this day.

The overhead lights burst with a pop. Darkness descended. Not even the light from the outside pierced the deep black that filled the room.

Nothing good would come of this.

CHAPTER THIRTEEN

SARAH

THAT WAS when all hell broke loose.

The room went pitch black. There was no light to be had, not even from the glow of the media equipment or the screens floating in the room.

There was a crack of glass breaking, the smell of smoke, and then a scream.

"Secure the king!"

Chaos erupted. Shouts and cries of distress came from the audience. Every karu—dozens—croaked loudly in warning.

Vekele moved to stand in front of her. His wings were out. He stood close enough that the wispy feathers brushed against her.

"Stay back," he ordered.

A shot pierced the noise of the room. Sarah had no idea how she heard the relatively quiet shot amid all the shouting and the dull thuds of people falling to the floor.

Vekele flinched and grunted.

"You're hit," she said.

"I said stay back." He flexed his wings, forcing her to step back.

Slowly, her eyes adjusted. She had just enough light to see figures moving in the dark. Only the perspective was wrong. Everyone stood extraordinarily tall. Granted, everyone on Arcos seemed to be taller than her, but this was taller than normal.

Ghost nosed her hand.

Understanding flooded through their bond. She saw through his eyes. Impressions of *pack* and *safe* twisted with the vision.

Someone grabbed her hard and yanked her, so she stumbled over her own feet. An arm clamped over her throat, pinning her back to someone's chest.

"Let me go!" she shouted.

"Quiet," a voice warned, moments before a slap landed across her face.

A punch to her flank followed, knocking the breath out of her, rendering her unable to think beyond the pain in her abdomen for a few moments. She scratched at the arm pinning her in place. She wasn't a fighter, with noodly arms and no muscle tone to speak of. Her feet flailed, kicking but striking nothing.

Ghost snarled and jumped at the attacker. Wooziness washed over her as Ghost's vantage clashed with what her body felt. A hand clamped over her mouth. No claws, so probably a man. Ghost's teeth sank into her attacker's arm.

The attacker released Sarah. She scrambled away, disoriented by the noise and what she saw through Ghost's eyes. The edge of the signing table dug into her hip. Smoke stung her eyes.

A kick landed on Ghost's ribs. He squealed in pain.

"Stop! He's a baby," she said. Desperate for any sort of weapon, she groped around the table. She knocked over one of the vases stuffed with flowers.

She hefted the vase over her head and brought it down on the man who kicked Ghost. He staggered back, clutching his head. She swung the vase again. It was heavier than it looked.

This time, it shattered on impact.

The man growled, clearly infuriated. He seemed to grow taller. Darker. He had wings, but not the feathery angelic sort that Vekele sported. These seemed leathery, like a bat. What little light there was gleamed on the vicious talon on the wingtip.

They swiped at her. She jumped back, tripping over a fallen chair and landing on her ass. She scrambled backward, her shoes sliding across the polished floor.

Pitch screeched, diving directly for the man's head. He shouted, arms waving to fend off the massive bird.

Sarah crawled to the table, hiding partially under the cloth. The air was easier to breathe near the floor. Was it gas or smoke from a fire? She couldn't tell.

"Princess, with me," a woman said, tearing away her hiding place. Sarah recognized her as one of the king's guards, Kenth.

Sarah climbed to her feet, coughing from the smoke.

They made it exactly two steps before Kenth staggered and crumpled to the floor.

"No, no. Please be okay," Sarah said, pressing her hand to the spreading stain on the woman's front. She was unresponsive but breathing. There was so much blood. Where were the guards? The king?

"Someone help us!" she shouted, looking frantically in the darkened room for assistance. Instead, she found a nightmare.

Vekele was fighting off two attackers. He moved with mesmerizing grace, blocking blows, and getting his own hits in.

He spun, wing raised to block, and spun again to strike. He kicked low, missing his opponent's leg. The other attacker landed a blow to his shoulder in the sensitive area between his wings. Two against one wasn't fair odds, and he could not keep the pace up forever. They had weapons. Vekele only had his fists.

Ghost nipped at her hand, grabbing her attention. Danger coursed through their bond.

It's all danger in here.

A figure emerged from the gloom, standing directly in front of Vekele. Too close. They raised a pistol. At that distance, it would be impossible to miss.

The figure raised the pistol, the barrel gleaming in the poor light.

"No!" She couldn't lose another person she loved. Not again. Her heart wasn't strong enough. She threw out a hand and something... *odd*... happened. Something inside her, the same thing that felt like Ghost, pulled.

An inky black tendril rose from the gloom and swiped at the attacker, knocking the pistol to one side.

The shot missed Vekele. Relief flooded through her.

As quickly as it appeared, the tendril vanished.

Sarah's knees gave out, her body suddenly too heavy to stand upright.

What was that?

Vekele caught her by the elbow, preventing her from collapsing.

VEKELE

"Hold on to Ghost," Vekele said. That was all the warning he gave before scooping her up into his arms. There was no time for formalities. Sarah held onto Ghost, still snarling and trying to climb over her shoulder to tear out the throat of the nearest non-pack member, a sentiment he shared.

Vekele's wings wrapped around them, creating a barrier, and he ran. He powered through the crowd, knocking people aside. Someone struck him from behind and he stumbled, nearly dropping her and Ghost. Pitch swooped down, talons extended, and attacked. A blade nicked his wing near the base, not deep enough to damage it, but enough that he would tire quickly.

This needed to be over. Now.

He burst onto the balcony into the sunlight, free of the choking darkness. Without hesitation, he hopped over the railing and fell.

They fell for a heartbeat. His wings unfolded and caught the air, slowing their descent to the plaza below. Unbalanced as he was, this was not a controlled glide. They were falling too fast. He banked to the right to avoid crashing into the building. Sarah twisted in his arms, peering over his shoulder at the chaos they left behind.

"You said you couldn't fly!" she shouted over the wind.

"This isn't flying. This is falling."

The ground rushed toward them. He bent his knees, preparing to land hard.

He staggered on impact, but he did not drop his mate. She wiggled out of his hold, and Ghost jumped down to the ground. The void beast growled at an unseen foe and took off at a run.

"Ghost! Where are you going?" Sarah called.

"There is no time. We must leave." They were exposed on all sides. Empty, the plaza had been cordoned off for the ceremony. A pair of flyers—most likely belonging to the royal guard—waited on the far side of the plaza.

"But Ghost—"

"Will find you." He took her hand and pulled her toward the nearest flyer.

Vekele recognized the flyer as a short-range model and lacked enough fuel to go anywhere Vekele considered a stronghold. The flyer was not ideal, but good enough to get away.

Ghost returned; his muzzle bloodied but otherwise intact. Somewhere, Vekele suspected, an enemy writhed in pain.

"Good male," he said, reaching down to pat the void beast. Ghost took a step back, then allowed the touch, bumping the top of his head to Vekele's palm.

The hatch on the nearest flyer was secure. He could force the lock but did not wish to waste time. Growling in frustration, he slammed his hand against the keypad.

A shot pinged off the back of the flyer. Sarah flinched, crouching down. "Hurry up and open it."

"I lack the code, and it will take too long to force."

Her eyes widened in astonishment. "You're stealing a spaceship."

"I am a prince. This is an emergency requisition, and this vehicle is not capable of spaceflight."

She snorted, quietly laughing. "Oh, you're serious."

"They would be compensated." Their survival was more important than worrying about property.

Another shot. Sarah jumped, her eyes turning black.

"All will be well," he said. "Do not panic."

"Don't lie to me. How about that one?" Sarah pointed across the plaza to a two-seater model with the hatch open.

The flyer would suffice, but they would be exposed.

"Stay close. Do not run in a straight line. Veer left and right," he said.

"Zig-zag. Got it."

He grabbed her hand and ran, shielding them with his wings. Pitch flew ahead, finding the best path. He moved to the right, bullets kicking up shards of pavement. His wings stung as debris bounced off.

"In," he shouted, lifting Sarah up and into the vehicle. "Stay down."

She slid low in the seat, curling her body around Ghost.

Vekele jammed himself into the pilot's seat. His wings occupied an uncomfortable amount of room. Logically, he should call them back, but he was too agitated. They were attacked. His mate had blood on her. They were not out of danger yet.

He forced open a panel and tugged on wires.

"You really are hot -wiring a car. We're stealing a car," she said.

"Now is not the time. We can debate the morality of this when we are safe." He pinched two wires together and punched the starter with more force than necessary.

The engine came to life.

He engaged the anti-grav, and the flyer rose off the ground. The shell slowly rose, sections unfurling and closing over the open vehicle.

"We're stealing a flying car," his mate said. "It's wrong that this is the best thing ever."

"It is a personal flyer, and not a very nice one."

"Well, beggars can't be choosers." She laughed again, a frantic edge in the sound.

Vekele leaned over and placed his hand on the back of her neck. "All will be well."

She took a shaky breath. "I left Kenth bleeding out on the floor. All those people—"

"We are targets. The best thing we can do is remove ourselves from the crowd. That will keep the most amount of people safe." He hoped. Kenth's injury was troubling. Baris had not been in the crowd. Hopefully, that meant the royal guards removed him promptly and Kenth had returned to retrieve Vekele and Sarah.

An attack on the palace. The amount of planning required to bypass the many levels of security was astounding. Someone in the guard had to have been compromised. Who had betrayed them?

The computer chimed, the engine ready for flight.

"Fasten the safety harness," he said.

"Can you even fly this?"

"My vision is not perfect, but the navigation system will compensate."

"I meant, like, do you know how to fly?"

"I am proficient and passed training," he replied.

"I took driver's ed, too, but that doesn't mean I can properly handle a bus."

Vekele ignored her chatter. In the time they spent at Summerhall, he learned that her chatter was directly linked to nervousness.

He needed to focus. While the navigation system helped to avoid collisions, it was not perfect and slow to respond at high speed. They needed to leave. Now.

He picked a direction at random. The small vehicle could not travel off the planet. Fuel also limited their flight range. He needed to find a safe location to regroup.

The flyer rose, one of several fleeing the palace, and streaked across the sky.

CHAPTER FOURTEEN

SARAH

"Exit the vehicle," Vekele ordered.

Sarah unbuckled the safety harness, her hands shaking. Ghost kept bumping his head against her head, whining. "I know, I know. We're okay," she said, repeating the words in a desperate attempt to make it true.

"We are safe for the moment," Vekele said. He reached across the cramped space and opened a compartment. His wings took up most of the cabin space. "Take this kit. Inside is disinfectant and a cleansing cloth. Clean yourself and Ghost. I will disable the tracking on this flyer."

Right. That sounded sensible. Responsible. She was grateful that Vekele took the lead. She didn't have to think, only follow orders. Unfortunately, that left plenty of space in her head for memories of the shouts and screams to play on repeat.

Sarah took the pack and climbed out of the ship. In the fresh air, she still smelled the smoke. It clung to her.

"This is shock," she said, stumbling on shaking legs.

People died right in front of her. Kenth fell to the floor. Her blood still coated Sarah's skin.

Ghost leaned into her, the touch grounding her. She stroked his fur, soft as silk and wispy as fog. He was hurt, most likely bruised ribs, having caught a kick meant for her. The kit had a medical scanner. Sarah fumbled with the device, managing to turn it on but unable to do more than that.

Frustrated, she threw it to the ground. Ghost rested with his head on his paws, unconcerned. Through their bond, she sensed he was tired, and his ribs ached, but he was unbothered by the pain.

She sat on the damp grass next to Ghost, stroking his soft fur. She didn't like being unable to take proper care of him. Ghost got hurt protecting her and she should be able to make him more comfortable. Or take him to a vet at the very least.

Night sounds surrounded them. A cool breeze brought fresh scents of trees and vegetation. It had rained recently, and the air held onto a chill. A familiar stone temple loomed in the distance.

"Looks like we brought you home," she said. Slowly, too slowly, the tension drained. The shouts and cries of pain faded. The scent of recent rain replaced the stench of blood. She dumped the kit onto the ground but couldn't make herself do much of anything.

Vekele took the cloth from her hand. He knelt in his customary spot off to the right, putting her in his field of vision. With his black wings out, he looked like a dark angel.

Without saying a word, he cleaned off the gore on her. Tenderly, he worked the cloth around her fingers, getting dried flakes of blood out from underneath her fingernails. The cloth carefully wiped her face. He lifted her hair to get the back of her neck. His touch was firm but gentle, warm, and alive.

When the cloth was dirty, he snapped it twice, and the dirt dissolved. That was a neat trick, and she'd want to know more, but not right then. All she wanted was to feel his hands on her.

As the cloth made another pass on her face, she grabbed his wrist. "You're being sweet, but I don't want you to be sweet right now," she said.

"Tell me what you need." His wings flexed, and his lips curled back in a smug grin. He absolutely knew what she needed.

Sarah grabbed him by the fabric of his shirt and leaned forward. Her mouth slammed against his. In an instant, his arms wrapped around her, holding her to him. His lips yielded to hers, opening and allowing her tongue to sweep inside. For a man unfamiliar with kissing, he was a quick study. He was a pro-level kisser. Topnotch.

"I need you to be naked. Right now," she said.

"Sarah, you could be injured."

"I'm not." She felt lots of ways—shaky, stressed, on the verge of an adrenaline crash, trapped in a nightmare—but none of those were due to an injury.

"I will not know for sure until I inspect you," he said in his stubborn, princely voice. Protesting that she was fine would only drag out the process. He would not be deterred.

"Fine. Start here." She tapped her lips.

His head tilted, trying to see her.

"Here." She grabbed his hand and pressed it to her lips. "Better kiss me again and make sure I'm not injured there."

He made a rumbling noise, half-amused and half-annoyed. The kiss was perfunctory.

"You did it wrong," she said.

"Did I?" Definitely amused.

"You really got to get in there and check the whole situation out."

"Show me," he ordered.

Sarah moved closer, straddling his lap, and leaned closer for another kiss. This one started slowly, deepening and heating with each heartbeat. His hands settled on her hips, holding her in place.

His head dipped down to her neck. Teeth nipped at her ear lobe. He kissed a trail down to her shoulder.

"This is highly inefficient," he said.

"I agree. Help me get this dress off." She moved to sit on her knees, and he yanked the dress off over her head. Cool air surrounded her. His hands roamed over her stomach and hips, clinical in their touch. Once satisfied that she was uninjured, the strokes grew into caresses.

"You're wearing too many clothes," she said, tugging his shirt open. Buttons popped off.

"I have not finished inspecting you." His hands caressed her arms.

Honestly, it was sweet, but so frustrating. She grabbed his hand and shoved it against her pussy. "Here. That's where it hurts."

He ground the base of his palm against her. She rocked up into the touch. He chuckled. "Is this what you need, my mate?"

"Yes. Please, Vekele." She wasn't above begging. She wanted to chase away the memories of the day and lose herself in the pleasure they shared. "I need you."

"You need me here?" A finger stroked her slick flesh, skimming over her clit.

"Yes," she moaned.

"All of me? Are you going to take both my cocks?"

"I want them. All of you." Just one of his dicks was enough of a challenge. Two dicks at once would be like climbing Everest. It might kill her, but she was going to try.

He worked a finger into her, then two. She rode his hand, letting him work her open. Her arms hooked over his shoulders, allowing her fingers to dig into his wings. They were soft and insubstantial, nothing more than a whisper of a touch. He groaned as she grabbed the wing base. The wings shuddered and flexed.

"Yes, there," he said. His eyes, drawing the darkness into them, closed in bliss.

With only a growl as a warning, he pushed her onto her back. The hard ground knocked the breath out of her. Grass tickled her between her shoulder blades.

He stretched above her, his eyes black as any void, and wings stretched wide, framed by starlight. He was magnificent.

VEKELE

He was as clumsy as a hatchling. Fumbling with the opening of his trousers. Throwing his mate to the ground like an equipment pack.

She smiled up at him, her red hair fanning out against the grass, oblivious to his failings.

"If you are in pain, you will tell me to stop," he said.

"Yes." She tugged him down for another kiss.

This close, at this angle, she was just the impression of color, the suggestion of a shape. It was not good. He needed to see his mate. He needed to see the ecstasy on her face when he took her.

He pushed into her slowly, feeling her stretch around him. She was tight, and it would be a tighter fit for all of him. He'd stretch her further before they were finished. A few shallow thrusts and he nearly lost himself. She raised her hips, meeting him.

She was everything. More than he ever dared hope for himself, and he came too close to losing her that day. Someone attempted to take her from him.

With a firm grip on her hips, he sat upright. Her legs wrapped around him, and she reclined on his thighs, her shoulders on the ground but her hips in his lap.

He needed to be inside her, all of him, to possess her.

"You will take all of me," he said. "Do not be concerned. I will prepare you."

He rubbed the sensitive bundle of nerves she called her clit. Her response was immediate, clenching around him and lifting her hips with a mew of desire. She liked that. He continued to rub, working his length in and out slowly.

"Good. Look how you want more," he said. Praise rolled off his tongue as he worked a second finger into her channel.

She hissed, her body tense and still. After a heartbeat, she relaxed. "That's so good," she moaned. Another finger, working them in and out until he could be sure that she could take him.

"Are you ready, my love?" he asked.

She nodded, biting her lower lip.

"Tell me," he said.

"Yes, my prince."

Joy and adoration swelled inside him. His princess. His mate.

He lined his second cock up and pushed in. The tight heat of her surrounded him. "My princess," he groaned.

With an arm around her waist, he lifted her upright. She gasped at the new position. He held still, letting her adjust. Her arms went over his shoulders, back to the base of his wings. Fingers dug in, sending sparks along the sensitive flesh there.

He rocked up into her. His wings wrapped around them, sheltering them. She rose and fell on his shaft, her mouth open and panting. His sweet mate. Her fingernails scratched at his back. A thrill went through him, wanting to wear her mark. Then everyone would know he belonged to her. No one would dare try to take her from him.

With a groan, he pushed her to her back. His hips gained speed, pumping in and out at an erratic pace. Her cries of bliss filled the night. The tight coil of pleasure spiraled inside, racing up his spine. Soon it would consume him.

He lifted her legs, changing the angle, and thrusting harder. Her body tensed, and her channel tightened and squeezed as she reached her climax.

She was beautiful as pleasure took her.

He pushed into her twice, three times, more, and found his release. He felt hot and cold all at once and utterly content.

He collapsed onto his forearms, keeping his weight off her. His forehead pressed against hers.

"My princess, my love," he whispered.

"My arrogant prince," she whispered back. "Don't you dare almost die again."

He swallowed back the urge to deny the danger they had been in, specifically when he had been cornered. He saw the tendril that Sarah conjured.

"You saved me," he said.

"I can't lose you, Vekele. I can't do that again," she said.

He pulled back far enough to see her properly. Her eyes glistened, as if ready to cry. He could not make the promise she wanted to hear, that they would never be in danger. That he would never leave her. It was a dangerous world and, he suspected, about to get more dangerous soon.

"You were brought here for me," he said, his confidence —though his mate would call it arrogance—returning. "I pity those who try to take me from you."

THE NIGHT TURNED COLD, and sense returned to them.

"You're bleeding," Sarah said, carefully touching his upper arm.

He twisted to look. Blood had soaked through the fabric. He did not remember the injury. "A graze."

"Off," she said, snapping her fingers. "Come on, get it off."

He blinked at the audacity.

"Don't look at me like that. Undress so I can clean it and put goop on it."

"I see you are flaunting your vast medical knowledge with such detailed technical terms," he said. Still, he removed the shirt. His shoulders protested at the movement, and the fabric peeled away painfully where it had dried.

"Well, you've got enough energy for a smart mouth, so you're not dying," she said in a dry tone.

"I have enough energy to fuck you senseless *and* have a smart mouth, thank you very much."

She clicked her tongue in a gesture that seemed both mocking and amused. "Well, that's me told. Is there a light in the kit?" She rummaged through the emergency kit.

Vekele retrieved the lantern. Stored as a flat disc, it expanded into a globe and hovered a measure off the ground.

"That is a cool trick," Sarah said.

He handed her two packets, one a disinfectant and the other a gel to cover the wound.

Gently, Sarah dabbed at the injury. It burned slightly, but not worse than the actual shot. Her attention was soft and kind. Caring, even loving. No one had given Vekele such care since his parents' death. When they were alive, the king and queen remained aloof. He knew they loved him, but they had never been affectionate with little touches or soft words.

Sarah had both, but also had sharp looks and cutting comments. She had enthusiastic smiles and unabashed glee.

She had not said the word yet—love—but he felt it. His love for her grew moment by moment. Her care, her concern, all her actions led him to believe that she felt the same. She did not have to say the words. He knew.

It was... odd to be the focus of so much. Concern. Love. He craved it. Wanted every drop of it.

With her attention focused on his arm, he did his own inspection. The beginning of a bruise blossomed on her abdomen. He wanted to kill the male who dared to hit his mate, but that male was already deceased.

Vekele would have to be satisfied with hunting down the traitor who orchestrated the attack. Instinct— or perhaps a lifetime of mistrust— pointed to his aunt. *Cassana*. It had not escaped his attention that his dear, beloved aunt was absent from the signing ceremony.

The Starshade representatives had also been absent.

One coincidence was merely a coincidence. Two was a clue. Three was proof of conspiracy.

He did not know what the third coincidence was, but he knew he would find out easily enough.

"This is worse than a graze," Sarah chided as she applied the gel.

The sting of the medicated gel dragged his thoughts to the present.

"It is fine. I should have been gentler with you," he said, his fingers brushing against her stomach.

"I'm okay."

"You always say that when it is not true." He activated the scanner. The device was not programmed for human physiology, but it was the best he could do until they found a medic.

"Am I going to make it, doc?"

"You are far too glib about your survival," he grumbled. "No major organs are ruptured."

"Scan Ghost, please. He took a kick to the ribs."

The void beast slinked out of the shadows and allowed Vekele to scan his person.

"His ribs are bruised but not fractured. I can administer a pain medication if he wishes," Vekele said.

She squinted her two eyes, sensing the beast's choice through the bond. "He doesn't trust you right now. I think that's a no."

Vekele huffed. The beast barely tolerated him on a good day. They had an uneasy truce, but the assassination attempt was too much for the young creature. "That is understandable."

Sarah picked up her discarded garment and dressed reluctantly. In the lantern's glow, dark patches of dried blood stained the once vibrant fabric.

"There may be something suitable in the emergency kit. Stay here."

"Isn't this the emergency kit?" she asked.

"One of three."

He retrieved two additional packs. These came standard with all flyers, even the ridiculously short-ranged ones like the one he stole.

No, requisitioned.

The larger pack contained a sleeping mat, blankets, and a pop-up shelter. It also had a pair of basic flight suits. They were not fashionable, but they were clean and warm. The smaller pack contained rations and water.

He ignored the emergency beacon. No one needed to know their location at the moment.

Dressed and fed, they crawled into the tent. She snuggled next to him on the sleeping mat and pressed a kiss to his cheek.

"Good night, sweetheart. Don't you dare get hurt again," she said, the yawn softening her threat.

He loved her so much his heart hurt from the enormity of it.

The king made a bargain to send her back to Earth if possible, and he agreed. Vekele had always believed himself to be an honorable male. For the first time, he wanted to break his vow.

He would keep his mate any way he could, even if he had to chain her to his bed again.

CHAPTER FIFTEEN

SARAH

"For a male who says he does not like trouble, you find plenty of it," Kenth said, striding down the ship's ramp.

Four additional guards followed. Their uniforms were stained and disheveled after a long night. Kenth wore the same uniform as yesterday, complete with bullet hole and bloodstain. Among the guards, Sarah recognized Luca, the guard who took her phone for examination.

"You're alive!" Sarah rose to her feet, stiff and all her muscles aching. Last night's promise of a bruise turned into a deep violet splotch covering her hip and part of her stomach, matching the ones on her arms. Honestly, the busted lip and swollen cheek hurt worse.

Ghost crowded in front of Sarah, pressing into her to get her to back up. He growled, his shadows doing a *thing*. He appeared twice his size and full of menace.

Pitch swooped down to land on Ghost's back. The karu stretched her wings and shrieked.

That was new. Sarah had no idea if Pitch cried for war or wanted Ghost to chill.

"Princess?" Concern sounded in the guard's voice.

"They're friends," Sarah said, her hand on the back of Ghost's neck. The bond felt stronger with touch. From his end, she felt a surge of *protect* and *pack* and *strangers*. Sarah sent a message of calm. They knew Kenth. They liked Kenth.

Ghost relaxed but remained close. Pitch returned to Vekele's shoulder.

Kenth marched straight up to Vekele. "She needs a medic. How irresponsible you are to enjoy camping in the wilderness when your mate is..." She waved a hand at Sarah's face. "Turning those colors."

"I am well. Thank you for your concern," he replied in a dry tone. "Scans indicated minimal damage to soft tissue. She has taken anti-inflammatory medication. What more could I do? Fly her directly to the capital and meet the assassins at a medical facility?"

They stared at each other, both tense and exhausted. Vekele needed a solid day's sleep, and Kenth looked like she had clawed her way out of a grave, complete with dirt under her talons.

This wasn't helpful.

Sarah placed a hand on Vekele's arm, letting him know her position. "I'm fine, all things considered. Vekele was shot, but it was superficial. What happened to you? I'm sorry I left you—"

Kenth dismissed her concern with a wave of her hand. "As was proper. Protocol in that situation is to remove members of the royal family and retreat to a secure location. Is this secure, Your Highness?" She turned her sharp gaze back to Vekele.

"I disabled the tracker on the flyer. No one found us until I messaged you," he said.

The other guard, Luca, inspected the flyer. "Doesn't this belong to Councilor Raelle?"

"Does it?" Vekele huffed, sounding amused.

"The councilor will be delighted to have assisted the prince," Kenth said. "Have you followed the news reports?"

"Not for more than a year," Vekele said.

"The king is missing."

A long moment passed. Vekele remained motionless. "You removed him. I heard—"

"That was not my order or my guards. They were imposters," Kenth said.

"A hostile force infiltrated the palace, the royal guards —" Anger flooded his voice. Pitch gave an agitated croak, full of frustration.

"You will have my resignation once we locate and retrieve the king," she said.

"How is Baris *missing*? He is the one person in the entire kingdom who cannot vanish."

"The king's signature has not left the palace, but I have been unable to reach him with the communication network. We have been locked out and no longer have control of the palace." Kenth spoke in such a brusque manner, Sarah wondered if this sort of thing happened every day.

Perhaps it did. Wasn't that what Vekele warned her about? His family played at murder and intrigue like it was a common family game night occurrence.

"If the king no longer lives…" Kenth said, her voice trailing off with meaning.

"Then I am king," Vekele responded. He sighed and scrubbed a hand over his face. Pitch gave a mournful croak. "Let us discuss this inside. My mate requires sustenance."

Sarah didn't know if her stomach could tolerate a meal, but she followed Vekele and the others onto the ship.

Ghost continued to guard her, but he did not growl. His snaps were reserved for those who strayed too close to them.

"This is familiar," she said. She wasn't sure what she had expected from the spaceship, maybe something like a miniature flying palace, all gold ornaments, and lush interiors. The ship was stark. Amber light strips along the wall softened the utilitarian gray interior. The space felt clean but impersonal.

"It is what I used to transport you from Miria to Summerhall," Vekele said, striding down a corridor.

"This is the king's personal ship," Luca said, pride in his voice. "It has the most advanced engine in the fleet, capable of jumping hundreds of lightyears. We have cabin space for a large crew and guests, but it can operate with a minimal crew. There is a full-service galley capable of entertaining the finest guests—"

"Enough," Vekele snapped. "It is a very nice ship. We are all suitably impressed."

In the full-service galley, Vekele made breakfast while Kenth apprised him of the situation. Injuries: many. Fatalities: six, not as many as would be expected. A small explosive device disabled the power. A gas canister had been deployed just as someone with a karu symbiote cloaked the room in darkness. Considering the size of the room, multiple people were involved in creating the utter darkness that added to the panic and confusion. In the chaos, the assailants captured the king, attempted to take Sarah, and tried their best to kill Vekele.

By the time Kenth had been transported to a medical facility, the palace command codes had been changed, isolating the king with his captors.

Vekele set a bowl of porridge in front of Sarah. It wasn't great, but it tasted better than the chewy bars from the emergency kit.

"This is the work of the Starshades," he said.

"Why would the family attempt to assassinate you and abduct the king days before the wedding?" Luca asked. "That makes no sense."

"It is obvious. It is in their interest to remove me and my mate before we can produce a child with a claim to the throne."

Sarah stared down into her bowl of porridge, a blush burning fiercely on her cheeks. They hadn't discussed children, but they sure did all the things to make one. If they could. Could they?

She glanced at Vekele like he could answer that.

"They have every intention of keeping the king alive long enough to produce an heir. Once they have their heir, the king will meet with an unfortunate accident," Vekele said, his tone implying that anyone should understand the situation.

"Surely they can't expect the king to go through with the wedding now," Sarah said.

"They could coerce him. Convince him it is better to be their captive than whatever destruction they threaten," Vekele answered.

Sarah couldn't imagine what scenario would convince a king to marry the person who plotted the assassination of his brother and sister-in-law days before the wedding. She felt a certain kind of way about it, considering she was the nearly assassinated sister-in-law.

"Like bombing a city?" It was the worst thing she could think of.

"To spare innocent lives, yes," he said.

Sarah had only met Baris once in private. The other few times were in front of an audience. She did not know him at all, but that sounded like the man she met in the gardens at Summerhall.

"It is Lady Cassana," Kenth said. "She has access to the palace, knowledge of the security systems, its weaknesses…" Her lips twisted like the words left a bad taste in her mouth. "And the habits of the guards. She has had years to study the palace layout and find the best route to smuggle in her mercenaries."

"She has no access codes," Vekele replied.

"I flatter myself when I say the security systems are robust, because I designed them, but any network can be compromised," Luca added. "Even mine."

"The king remains at the palace, which points to Lady Cassana as the mastermind. Even if she compromised the security system and took over the network, she is still confined to the palace."

"How?" Sarah asked. "If she controls the network—"

"It is a different system," Vekele said. "Only Baris or I can release her shackles."

She found that unlikely. "And your brother is incapable of being coerced?"

Vekele's lips pressed together. "It does not matter. Baris is at the palace. We go there."

VEKELE

"This is all we could muster?" Vekele frowned at the tablet.

"That is every garrison able to respond in an hour," Kenth said.

"It will do." They needed to act now. If they waited, Cassana would cement her hold over the palace and convince Baris to do something foolish.

Like marry that traitor Joie Starshade.

They were exhausted and injured. Rushing could be disastrous but waiting for reinforcements meant they would face even more unfavorable odds.

It had to be now.

He and Kenth coordinated with the garrisons and guards still in the capital. A direct assault proved impossible. They had to be devious.

"There are disused utility tunnels under the palace," Vekele said, highlighting the tunnels on the screen.

"Those are sealed," Kenth said.

"Not all entrances. Here and here. Those connect with the capital's stormwater and sewer system. Baris and I discovered these when we were children." Vekele pointed to the two unsecured entrances.

Through the bond, he got the distinct impression that Pitch did not want to go into the tunnels. He reached up to stroke her beak. She caught his finger in her talon and croaked, too cranky for affection. He understood the sentiment.

"Princes should not play in sewers," Kenth said, scandalized by the prince's youthful misbehavior.

"I apologize for the personal insult, but it serves us now. We enter here. Luca has the skills to bypass any codes. Kenth, you will coordinate from the ship. Sarah, you will remain with Kenth."

Sarah opened her mouth, as if to protest, then nodded. "Is there anything I can do? Let me help."

"You will help by remaining in a secure location, so I will not worry," he said. Her eyebrows drew together in that way that declared her unhappiness, but he spoke the truth. He could not afford to be distracted.

"I will need extra eyes on the screens, Princess Sarah," Kenth said.

"I can do that."

The rest of the plan fell into place. It was reckless. Rash. They did not have enough equipment or guards.

They waited in low orbit for the rest of the guards to arrive.

"Are you certain this is the way?" Sarah asked, placing a hand on his arm.

He blinked, tearing himself away from the tablet in his hands. Footage of the disastrous signing ceremony replayed. "I must—"

"Do *you* have to go?"

He tensed. If she thought him incapable, because of his injury—

"Because there's only one Prince Vekele. I happen to be very fond of that guy—"

"Very fond?"

She smiled, teasing and tempting. "*Very* fond, but he's also a leader, so maybe running through sewers all gung-ho isn't the best idea he's ever had."

"Your words are nonsensical."

"I mean, I'm worried. About you." She jabbed a finger against his chest. "I don't like it."

"But you like me. You are *very fond* of me."

"Because I like you." Strain and exhaustion were woven through her voice.

He placed a hand on the back of her neck and brought their foreheads together. He wanted her love. He wanted her heart, but he would accept her soft words that spoke around emotion: care and fondness.

He breathed, memorizing the scent of his mate in this moment, the sound of her beating heart, and the heat of her.

"I care for you," she said, her voice softer now. "Don't leave me."

"I need to do this."

"You're not the only one."

His grip tightened. If any of the guards observed them, he cared not. The world drifted away to be nothing more than distant noise. There was only him and his mate in this moment. He said, "I need to prove that I can. That I am not useless."

"You're not, and you know it. A useless man did not save my life last night."

"I know the tunnels. I am needed."

"There are maps."

This argument would go in circles for ages. Both were too stubborn to back down. Vekele saw only one way to end this.

"I have been hiding for so long," he said. "I refuse to hide any longer."

Speaking the words lanced the poison inside him. He felt freer. Lighter.

Sarah's shoulders relaxed. "Okay, but you have to come back to me."

"As you command, my princess."

THIS WAS TOO EASY.

They avoided detection as they accessed the tunnels. Security systems in the tunnels had not been upgraded in decades. A spotty network remained, easily confused into ignoring the two dozen guards, to say nothing about the gaps in coverage. Honestly, the security system was an outrage.

Pitch flew ahead, scouting his way even as her agitation soured his mood. The karu did not like the tunnels.

Being underground was wrong. She wanted an open sky, not this stink of motionless air.

The closer they got to the palace, the more the tunnels split into smaller and smaller passages, creating a grid underneath the fountain of the palace. The guards split into three teams.

As they approached the first checkpoint, Luca produced a hard-shell kit containing the tools he needed to disable the security system. Vekele barely had time to check on the position of the guards when the barrier unlocked.

The male grinned with satisfaction. "Do not be alarmed. I designed the system. That is why it fell so quickly."

Vekele's team went up toward the king's location. Another team went to free any captives that may be held in the lower levels. The third team went to secure the palace's command center. If they worked quickly, the coordinated attack would stretch the occupying forces too thin and they would break.

Vekele looked forward to the breaking.

Pitch very much agreed. She sent a strong impression of snapping twigs in her beak.

They found guards, palace staff, civilians, and anyone else unable to flee, detained on the lower levels. No captors, though. The second team handled releasing the prisoners and seeing them safely out.

Vekele's team continued upward.

"The king is in the tower," a guard reported, eyes fixed on his screen.

On the ground floor, they passed signs of battle: soot on the walls and blood on the floor. Bullets riddled the walls. Furnishings had been overturned and broken. Debris littered the floors. An emergency alert played on repeat, filling every screen and speaker. The sound of three distinctive notes, followed by the flat drone of the computer-generated voice, echoed down the halls.

"Turn off the alert," Vekele ordered. The beginnings of a headache formed behind his eyes. Yesterday had been taxing, and the droning alert felt like a needle poking at him.

"Sir," Luca said, rushing to the nearest terminal. In short order, the alert ceased.

Silence fell.

The wrongness of the situation only increased. Beyond the destruction, the ground floor was empty. Not a soul.

As were the first and second floors. The same pattern emerged: signs of conflict between the royal guards and the traitors. Blood stained the floors, yet there were no bodies. Vekele wondered if the casualties had been locked in a cold storage room or if the conspirators had done the decent thing and evacuated the injured for medical care.

Mostly, he worried about what Baris conceded to get medical care for the injured.

"I do not like this," he muttered. Pitch scouted ahead, finding nothing but empty corridors and vacant rooms.

The palace had always been a hive of activity. Vekele disliked the constant noise of footfalls, opening doors, and the whispers of conversation. There was no solitude to be found. Even in the relative sanctuary of his private quarters, attendants pestered him for the most inconsequential reasons. It was impossible to be alone in the palace...

Where was everyone? The further they went, the more Vekele grew certain that he had fallen for a misdirection.

They reached the tower and the king's quarters with no complication. Doors unlocked at Luca's command. No major hindrances, but enough of a delay to prevent him from strolling casually through the empty palace.

Yes, this was a misdirection. The final room proved it.

After the guards forced the door open, Vekele strode into the king's private quarters. Empty.

"The king's signature is here," Luca said, eyes fixed on a handheld screen.

The source of the signal was apparent. Left on a neatly folded handkerchief, sitting on a table like an offering, rested a severed thumb.

SARAH

Waiting sucked balls. Yes, Sarah understood she wasn't a badass, fighty-type person with hands that were registered as deadly weapons. She couldn't help and would only get in the way or get herself killed. Fine. But sitting around with nothing to occupy her thoughts blew. Her mind kept creating scenarios of all the ways the rescue mission would go wrong.

Bombs. Bullets. Bears. Other bad things that started with B. Look, panic was doing all the thinking for her now and her panicky brain wasn't logical. There could be bears.

The farther the teams infiltrated the palace without resistance, the more convinced that a massive bear trap waited at the end as a final boss fight.

Ghost climbed into Sarah's lap, nosing at her hand.

"You're almost too big for this," she said, knowing full well that Ghost could be enormous, but she'd happily let him crush her lap. She stroked his fur, scratching behind his ears, and booping his nose. Satisfaction came through their bond.

"That is disturbing," Kenth said.

"He likes it." She touched his nose with a finger. "Boop."

"He is growling."

"Happy growling. He likes getting his boop button booped." She touched his nose again. His tongue lolled out the side of his mouth.

"Check the feeds," Kenth said, turning her attention back to the mission.

"All work and no play will make you go gray," Sarah said.

Kenth laughed, the unexpected noise filling the cabin. "You must vex the prince."

"He enjoys it."

"Yes, and I imagine he growls, too."

A laugh, mortified and amused, bubbled up in her. It was wrong to laugh. So many people had been hurt less than a day ago. People had died. Hell, Kenth had been injured. She still wore her bloody uniform.

"I'm sorry we left you," Sarah said. "Yesterday."

"You have apologized once for an event that was not your fault."

"You needed help, and we left you bleeding on the floor." Sarah didn't know how to make her guilt plainer. If she had done something, anything, people in the audience wouldn't have died. Robert wouldn't have died. If she had known his headache wasn't an ordinary headache, if she had insisted they go to the hospital, then he might have lived.

She failed him.

"The bullet that hit me was coated with a paralytic. You lack the physical strength to move my body," she said, her tone harsh. "Are you a medic? Did you have the antidote in your pocket?" She did not pause for Sarah to answer. "Then there is nothing you could have done. Prince Vekele removed himself and you from the situation, as was protocol. I would have given you that direct order if I had been able to speak. Do not concern yourself with this, Your Highness."

It took a minute for Kenth's words to sink in and recognize the title. "Please, call me Sarah," she said.

"Monitor the screens, Sarah. I need to know if anyone leaves the palace."

Reaching around Ghost, Sarah tapped the screen, switching between feeds around the palace. The cameras captured external areas, delivery zones, a lot in front of a warehouse or depot, and another lot. Empty. Empty. Empty.

A group of people hurried across a lot toward a spaceship. Armed guards surrounded two people. Sarah recognized the aunt, Cassana, at the back of the group. She didn't look pleased.

"I've got something," Sarah said, swinging the screen toward Kenth.

Kenth took one look at the screen and started barking orders.

Sarah knew why. On the screen, the king had his hand tied with a ribbon to the woman at his side.

CHAPTER SIXTEEN

VEKELE

"How did they evade us?" Vekele threw the broken shackles that once bound Cassana across the room. On the screen, footage of Baris marching onto a ship played on repeat. What good did replaying the footage do? It told him all he needed to know. His brother bound himself to Joie Starshade, for some unfathomable reason.

Pitch launched herself from his shoulder, but not before digging her talons into his mantle hard enough to feel. Perched high on a beam, she squawked at his outburst.

Spoiled hatchling came through their bond.

He regretted his tantrum. Such actions changed nothing and only tarnished his reputation. Still, he did not worry about his reputation. He worried for his brother's life.

"I only have four eyes," Kenth said.

"*Six*. You had six eyes on your task, and you failed," he snapped.

"Thanks for including me. So happy to be part of the team," Sarah muttered.

Kenth's jaw clenched. Her eyes blazed with fury, but she remained silent. Good. Vekele was not in the mood to hear excuses about how her orders were to monitor and coordinate. One person—two if he counted his mate—could not prevent an armed escort from smuggling Baris out of the palace.

Truthfully, he should have aborted the mission the moment he found the palace deserted.

No. Not while the tracker embedded in Baris' thumb indicated he was in the palace.

After discovering the severed thumb, it was placed in a preservation container in the hopes that it could be reattached. The odds of that being successful were not favorable.

"We failed because we underestimated Lady Cassana," Kenth said. "I take full responsibility for that. Palace security—"

"Enough," Vekele said. Anger kept him upright and alert, but soon that would fade and exhaustion would have him. The last two days had been extraordinarily taxing. His front eyes hurt, overexposed to harsh light and not rested. He waved to the screen. "And turn that off. We have learned all we can from it."

A male sitting at the console fumbled with the controls until the screens went blank.

"Do we have an ID on the ship?" Vekele asked.

"It is registered to the House of Starshade," Kenth said.

So much for the king's plan for peace between the houses.

He scanned the crowd of guards, all watching him and ready for orders. They were exhausted, and it showed. Their work started with the attack at the signing ceremony and had not ceased. While Vekele had removed his mate from danger, the palace guards remained to fight the assault. They had been locked out of their own network and their defenses used against them. They suffered the loss of friends and comrades.

Bloodied and bruised, they were ready for new orders, despite swaying on their feet.

"What we know is that the Starshades did not negotiate in good faith with the king. They conspired with Lady Cassana to compromise the palace's security and orchestrate yesterday's attack. Now they have captured the king and are removing him from Arcos to, presumably, a location in Starshade territory," Vekele said.

Unease shifted through the guards. The facts were uncomfortable but had to be faced.

"First, your performance yesterday was exceptional," Vekele continued. "The Starshades' assault could have been much more deadly. Should have been. I suspect the traitors behind the attack are disappointed at how many lives you saved. Well done."

The guards visibly perked, straightening their shoulders and lifting their chins.

"Several things must happen now," Vekele said. "We need a medic. Contact Harol and tell him to be ready to depart in an hour. Yes, I know there are palace medics ready now, but I trust Harol, and I am not inclined to put my faith in someone I do not trust at the moment."

A murmur of agreement rippled through the guards.

It felt good to have a mission and a purpose again. Familiar. Time away to recover and adjust to his injuries and new state of being had been necessary. Hiding himself away like he was a blight had been a mistake. Baris tried to tell him this in his heavy-handed, well-meaning way. It only took a second failed assassination attempt and abduction for Vekele to understand.

"We will rescue the king. Failure is unacceptable. This is the fastest ship in the kingdom. The Starshade ship is old and slow. It uses a tunnel drive." He looked to Luca for confirmation.

"We have a jump drive. We're three times as fast," Luca said.

"Wherever the Starshades go, we will be there. They cannot escape us." Even with their head start. Vekele had a working knowledge of the ship and understood some of the limitations. He would rely on the engineer and mechanic for the specifics. "This ship is long-range and faster, but the drive requires a long cooldown between jumps. We get one chance to intercept the Starshades. They must be headed to their territory in the outer reaches."

The navigator spoke. "There is an asteroid belt surrounding the Starshade home world. Jumping there would be risky. Without detailed maps and readings, we would risk landing in the wrong spot and the ship would be torn apart."

"How recently were our maps updated?" Vekele asked.

"Not recent enough for my liking," the navigator said. Such information was closely guarded while the houses warred with one another.

"Then we intercept them along their route. Give me locations."

Eyes fixed on screens, calculating the most likely scenarios. They would have the answer soon.

"They will desire to travel undetected," Kenth said.

"Black Space," Vekele said, having an entire conversation with Kenth with a handful of words.

"What's that?" Sarah asked.

"Unmarked territory. No network relays. No markers. If your navigation fails, you can be lost. Permanently," Kenth said. "Space is massive. It is easy to forget that when you have star charts."

To emphasize her point, she wiped away the screen with a wave of her hand and called up a chart.

"Here," she said. "It is a disused station. There is no traffic, but the station's network relay may still be operational. Using that as a marker is perfect for a vessel needing to travel undetected."

"I concur," the navigator said.

If they were wrong and the Starshades chose a different path, Vekele's crew would still be positioned to reach Starshade territory, albeit they would have to fight their way through the defensive perimeter. Successfully rescuing Baris would not be impossible, but it would be costly. Their best chance of success was to do it once and do it correctly.

"Very well. That will be our destination. I will take as many guards as we can fit into the ship. Contact the outer garrisons and send for reinforcements." He knew the reinforcements would be slow to arrive, but he would take what he could get. Turning to Kenth, he said, "You will remain here and secure the palace."

"Sir—" Kenth looked as if she would argue with him. She did not want to be left behind. He understood the sentiment.

"You are injured, and I know I ask much of you, but we must establish control at the palace. Enlist Councilor Raelle. She is ruthlessly efficient," he said, knowing that he needed to contact the councilor. He dreaded the call, but the council needed to be updated on the situation.

"Sir," she said, with a stiff nod.

"Good. I will leave you to decide who remains at the palace and who comes on the mission. However, if you are injured, you stay behind and get your ass to a medic. I want a complete ship's inventory. Weapons, ammunition, food, oxygen, medical gear, soap. Tell me how many specks of dust you find under the furniture. I want to land on my medic's front step and be in the stars in an hour. You have your orders."

The guards scrambled into action. There would be chaos on the ship until they left orbit.

He held out a hand to his mate. "Come with me."

"Am I counting dust bunnies?" Sarah asked, slipping her hands into his.

"You require a shower and rest."

"Same goes for you."

"When we leave orbit." There would be little to do once the journey began. He would sleep then. "We are commandeering the king's cabin."

SARAH

"What is that?" Vekele settled in next to her on the bed. It was comfortable and dominated the cabin, making the space feel small. After two days, the cozy charm had worn off and now the space felt confining. Hard to believe that this was the king's cabin. It wasn't utilitarian, but it lacked the over-the-top opulence Sarah associated with the king and the palace.

Spaceships played by different rules, apparently.

How weird was it that she was totally chill about being on a spaceship? She couldn't get her head around it. She watched the stars streak by outside the windows—not really windows, but what else could she call them?—for hours. There wasn't much in the way of entertainment on the ship. No Netflix. No one told her space travel was so boring.

The crew passed the time with card games. She even saw a Karu and Beast board set up. When she came over, eager to play, they all miraculously found tasks that needed to be done and left.

The only people who spent any time with her were Vekele and Ghost, who terrorized the crew into giving him treats and overly plump cushions. Vekele told the crew that Ghost was only dangerous if Sarah was threatened, but it didn't matter. Sarah imagined that a void beast nosing around the dinner table was as disturbing as a timber wolf begging for scraps and got the same response.

You gave the timber wolf what it wanted, and you got to keep all your fingers.

She hadn't seen much of Vekele in the last two days, either. The crew demanded much of his attention, plus there was hijacking the Starshade ship to plan. Whenever she did see him, a crew member would interrupt. Vekele slipped into bed late and left early. Rumpled sheets on his side of the bed were the only evidence that he slept at all.

She wasn't complaining. It was obvious how much he enjoyed being in command again. He'd spent his entire career in the military, on ships such as this. He was in his element, positively glowing with enthusiasm when discussing the armory or the ship's defensive capabilities. She was grateful to have him for a few hours all to herself.

Sarah leaned against him; his arm draped over her shoulder. "Luca transferred all my personal data from my phone to this tablet." The photos were thoughtful, but Sarah didn't need a copy of five hundred unread emails.

She scrolled through the photos. "This is my mom."

"Why do you display your blunt talons like that?" he asked, frowning at a photo of them showing off fresh manicures.

"We got our nails did," she said. Then added, "It's a beauty thing to paint our fingernails."

"To appear defenseless is a human standard?"

"No, it just makes me feel pretty."

He made a humming noise. "Are you considered pretty for human beauty standards?"

"I'm within conventional beauty standards," she answered, her tone teasing. "I got teased a lot when I was younger because I had a bad case of acne. Oh, that happens a lot around puberty with pimples on your skin."

"Puberty is unkind to all, it seems." He continued to flip through the photos.

Now she really wanted to see photographic evidence of awkward teen Vekele. Instead, she asked, "What about you?"

"Yes, I am pretty by Arcosian standards," he said. Despite the dry delivery, his lips quirked in amusement.

"Such modesty." She placed a hand over her heart. "I am humbled, Your Highness."

He removed her hand. "You do not call me that. Ever," he said. "I am your mate. There is no room for titles and honorifics between us."

Damn him for being sweet. "Okay," she said. "For the record, you're attractive according to human standards, too."

He said nothing, but a smug expression settled on his face. Oh, her prince was vain, and she loved it. Loved him.

Funny how that snuck up on her.

"What is your mother's name?" Vekele asked.

"Oh, Seraphina. I know, Sarah and Seraphina. I didn't pick my name."

"It is lovely. Does it have a meaning?"

"Seraphina is a type of angel… a divine being. They have wings."

"Like me?"

"Oh no, the last thing I need to do is feed your enormous ego."

He scoffed. "My ego is moderate, at best." Then, "My mother was called Annan."

"I like that. It's a good name." The photos progressively marched back into time.

"That's my friend Trisha," Sarah said, stopping at an image of her and Trisha standing in front of a yellow house. "We met in school. We used to go traveling together, but now she's married with a kid. That's the Emily Dickinson house. She was a poet."

"Your hair is the wrong color."

"That's my natural brown. Don't worry, it'll come back real soon. My roots are already showing," she said.

A weird sense of nostalgia fell over her. She missed Trisha and her family, but mostly, she missed the life she had years ago. Before everything soured and she hid away.

She paused at a photo of Robert.

Vekele tensed next to her, sensing the importance of this face. "That is him. Your mate."

He took the tablet, holding it close to examine Robert's face. It wasn't a particularly good photo. The flash washed out the color, and his eyes were closed, because he was always closing his eyes in photos. They had spent the day in Atlantic City, on the boardwalk, eating pizza and funnel cakes. Sarah could still smell the sea air and grease from the pizza place. A seagull had landed on the table. Being the softie he was, he fed it French fries rather than chase it away.

"I met Robert on my second day of college. He says we met at orientation, and we walked to the library together, but I honestly don't remember that." She wished she did. An extra memory of Rob sounded like a prize. "We had a class together and he sat next to me. I was eighteen, and I knew my life wouldn't be the same."

Vekele flipped to the screen to the next photo, carefully examining it. "I am sorrowful for your pain."

What else could he say? Sorry for your loss, but glad he's out of the way? No. Vekele wasn't like that. He said what he meant and never bothered to dress it up to spare feelings. That was his charm.

"Thanks," she said.

"Tell me about him."

"Hmm." She took the tablet back. "He'd like you. Love this whole situation, really. An adventure on an alien planet? Yes, please."

Sarah found herself sharing the story of their first date and how she didn't realize it was a date until he kissed her at the end of the evening. In her defense, they had friends in common and often went to dinner and the movies as a group of friends. One afternoon, he asked if she wanted to go to a movie; she thought they'd meet friends at the theater. Or at the diner. When no one showed up, she assumed they blew her and Robert off.

It wasn't her best moment. But that kiss…

She couldn't stop thinking about it. The next day, she texted him and asked him to please make it absolutely clear when they went on another date.

"He made notecards with what number date we were on and bullet points of the events planned," she explained, laughing at the absurdity of it.

Talking about Robert didn't hurt the way she expected. She'd barely spoken his name in three years and never talked about him. Well, she never talked about the good parts. Everyone wanted to talk about how it ended. But this? Laughing and sharing stories? She felt good. Lighter. More like herself than she felt in a long time.

"What about your brother?" she asked. "Tell me about him."

"You have met Baris," Vekele said.

"One time in private. The banquet doesn't count. He was being *the king* then."

"That is a fair assessment." He paused, considering his words. "Baris is overprotective. He has always been so, even when our parents were alive. More so after their deaths and we were confined to Summerhall."

He shared stories about midnight excursions to swim in the pond. How he and Baris tried to evade the security system that kept them prisoners. Once Vekele had been confined to bed with a fever for a week and Baris read aloud all the stuffy history books that Vekele loved and Baris found tedious.

"He is kind when he can be. Firm when he must be," Vekele said. Then, as an afterthought, "I believe you amuse him. He liked you."

She enjoyed listening to his stories. It was a hidden side of the stern prince that no one else got to see. She loved it when he joked, delivering it so dryly that no one believed he had a sense of humor. She loved how competitive he got when playing board games. She loved how he cooked for her, despite being a novice in the kitchen, and observed her reactions as she ate. She loved his dedication to his brother. She loved his stern daddy voice, never questioning that he should be obeyed.

He was different from Robert's goofy humor and laid-back attitude. Different, but similar in all the ways that mattered: thoughtful, loyal, and honest. New love hadn't erased old love. They sat together in her heart, the weight of them keeping her balanced and her soul satisfied.

Her decision was already made, wasn't it?

Sarah set the tablet aside and sat upright on the bed. "I don't want to go back to Earth."

"Your family—"

"I'll miss them, yeah, and I'd love to tell them I'm okay. Wouldn't it be wild if you could meet them? I know Baris said he would find a way to get me back to Earth —that was the bargain—but I'm not interested. I'm staying."

"Staying?"

"Staying," she agreed. "I mean, come on. Who was I fooling? I'm not leaving Ghost and you're not too bad, I guess—" She rolled her eyes, her tone dripping with sarcasm.

He pushed her onto her back and leaned over her, arms planted on either side of her head. She grinned up at him.

"Not too bad?" he asked. "You speak a hundred words to talk around the one I am desperate to hear."

"Desperate? I don't know what you mean." She totally knew.

"You know. Tell me."

"I love you," she said.

He grinned in triumph, like he claimed a prize.

Her, she realized. She was the prize.

"How fortunate, because I have decided that I love you," he said in his most imperious tone.

"I don't know how I got so lucky to find you, but I'm not letting you go," she said. Now that she confessed her feelings, the words wouldn't stop. "It's so improbable to find love once in a lifetime, let alone twice. How could I leave?"

He pressed his forehead to hers, and his eyes fluttered shut. For a moment, sweet and lush, there was only them. No brothers held hostage. No political games to play. No vendettas. Just Vekele and Sarah, as it should be.

"That is good," he said at last. "I had decided to chain you to my bed again rather than let you leave."

"Wow, that is super toxic and should piss me off, but why do I find it sweet?"

"Must be the ship's gravity. It is known to skew judgment." His lips hovered near hers, not touching. She moved up for a kiss, but he moved away. "How fortunate that I love you. You are more than I deserve. You are everything."

His mouth captured hers. The kiss started sweet, but quickly grew heated. He nibbled at her ears and kissed down her throat. He tugged at the bottom of her shirt, raising it to expose her stomach.

"Wait, let me." She removed her shirt.

He frowned at the mottled purple and green bruises. Tenderly, he brushed a finger over the discoloration. "I dislike that you were injured."

"I barely feel it now."

"I will make them pay." He leaned down, placing a soft kiss above her navel. "For every bruise, they will suffer. This is a broken finger." He kissed her hip, where the bruising was still a deep purple. "This will be a fractured hip."

His words were brutal, but they comforted her. "They're going to run out of bones for you to break," she said.

"Unlikely. There are several small bones in the inner ear. Those will be the bones of last resort." His fingers and lips mapped the bruising across her abdomen.

"Backup bones," she said, smiling and more than a little turned on. Well, Sarah learned something about herself that day. She was a bloodthirsty bitch.

Vekele hooked his fingers over the waistband of her sleep pants and panties, dragging them down. He settled onto his belly between her thighs.

The cabin door chirped. Someone wanted admittance.

"Ignore them," he ordered.

"I don't think we can." The interruptions had been steady all day. Their few hours of peace had been a fluke.

The door rang again. Whoever they were, they weren't going away.

"Prince Vekele? Your Highness? You're needed on the bridge," a voice said over the comms.

He groaned, rolling away. "The ship had better be on fire or I will have you scrubbing toilets."

"How long until we get there?"

"Three more days," he said.

Three more days of no privacy and no time together.

CHAPTER SEVENTEEN

VEKELE

THE STATION WAS AN INSULT. Stripped of useful parts, it was a hollow echo of its former self. Water dripped down some forgotten corridor. The air smelled musty. The lights flickered. He supposed he should count himself lucky that the station was habitable.

They did not have to be here long, just until the Starshade ship approached.

Guards carried supply crates off their ship. After days of being on the cramped ship, the crew would enjoy not being on top of each other.

Sarah's head constantly pivoted as she took in the sights. "Wow, this is something."

This station was a disgrace. It was beneath his dignity, and it worried him how much he wanted to dazzle Sarah with the riches of the Arcos kingdom.

The sound of dripping water grew louder.

The riches of the Arcos kingdom... *such as they were*, he mentally amended.

"It does not take much to impress you, Sarah of Earth," he said.

She leaned into him, nudging him with her shoulder. Compared to him, her form was too slender to cause injury or even move him. There was no reason for warmth to spread in his chest, no joy to be taken from her touching him voluntarily.

"Was that a joke? Are you giving me shit?" she asked.

He grimaced. "Absolutely not. Do humans do that?"

"What? No! No, that's just an idiom. It means giving me a hard time. Teasing me." She bared her teeth in that gesture that she assured him was friendly, despite being a universal signal of aggression.

Humans were odd.

Luca and the other guards kept their eyes forward, ignoring their banter.

He enjoyed the exchanges with Sarah. No one else dared to tease him or give him shit.

They reached a juncture. Luca pointed to the left, down a dark corridor. "The communication hub should be down there."

"If it has not long since been stripped for parts," Vekele said.

"We won't know until we look." Luca marched into the darkness. Sarah's void beast trotted after the female. Sarah moved to follow.

Vekele placed a hand on her shoulder, holding her back. "With me. Do not leave my side."

Their footsteps echoed down the corridor. His wings were out, shielding Sarah. Luca—the impertinent male — gave him a curious look.

Vekele lifted his chin. His instincts to protect Sarah were not to be questioned. She had suffered many injuries, and he would not have her injured again while she was in his care. It was simply a matter of good leadership and had nothing to do with the warm fluttering he felt when she flashed her ridiculous smile.

Like a hatchling practicing how to hunt.

Even with Pitch scouting ahead, Vekele did not relax until they reached the communication hub without incident.

He waited until Luca verified the instrument panel had what he needed, then ordered a pair of guards to search the station for anything useful. Once the crew had enough to keep them occupied and out of mischief, he left with Sarah to practice exerting her will over her bond.

He found a room large enough and clear of debris.

"Was this a greenhouse?"

"Hydroponics, for food and oxygen," he said. Racks formed orderly lines. Some were empty, the pod dry and barren. Others burst with uncontrolled growth, indicating a water leak. Overhead lighting was uneven, creating bright spots and deep wells of darkness. He said, "This is adequate. Call your beast. Proceed."

The void beast prowled the room, ignoring both of them.

"Ghost…"

The beast ignored her.

"Ghost, come here?"

"Issue a command. Draw him to you. Do not beg," he said.

Sarah huffed. "Ghost, come here."

An ear flicked, but the beast continued its circuit around the room.

"Draw him to you. It is simple. Even fledglings can draw on their shadows."

She ran a hand through her hair, tugging on her red locks. "Great, you're telling me kids can do this."

"You have done this before." He kept his voice even and controlled.

"Once and you were about to have a bullet in your head." She squeezed her eyes closed and stretched out her hands, her fingers grasping at some invisible thread. She ground her teeth together, nearly growling in effort.

Nothing. The shadows did not swell out of the dark corners of the room. The lights did not even dim.

She dropped her hand with an exasperated sigh.

"What is that?" he asked, unimpressed.

"Calling my shadow."

"No, that was... I do not know what that was. Watch me."

"I'm watching." She folded her arms over her chest and cocked a hip dramatically to one side.

Petulant. He knew a distraction when he saw one.

"No, you are looking, but you are not watching. See my marks," he said. He removed the overcoat and tossed it to the ground. Stripped down to his waistcoat and shirt, he rolled up the sleeve.

Lines of black ink shifted under his skin.

With his index finger, he touched his forearm. "Feel it," he said.

"I can see just fine."

Huffing, he placed her hand over the mark. This was a child's lesson. He needed to remind himself that she did not spend the first years of her life anticipating a bond with a karu.

"Feel," he repeated. "The parasite moves in clusters."

Her eyes went wide, but she did not remove her hand. "I feel…that's so gross. That's in me?"

"The lump that you feel under my skin is an illusion, nothing more than a phantom. Your eyes witness the clusters moving, so your brain fills in the sensory gap of feeling the cluster. Being able to feel the shadow within makes it easier to manipulate. It is a trick used by novices," he said.

"Okay. Mind over matter." She flexed her fingers and closed her eyes. "Seize the adventure."

While she muttered motivational phrases to herself, he studied her. Her hair was an offense to good taste and nature, but he had grown fond of the outlandish color. It suited her.

He liked how her plain beige skin displayed the royal mark on her arm. The fine details did not fade at the edges. They were crisp and sharp.

Shadow marks rose on the hand touching him. They were faint but present.

Shadows surged, wanting to envelop them, to protect his female, who was all at once a complication, both a captive and a gift.

His mate.

She cracked open an eye. "What? I did it wrong."

He swallowed. "No. You did well."

"Then what's that look for?"

"I enjoy looking at you."

She rolled her eyes—still a disturbing sight, but he resisted the urge to shudder. "This is pointless. I can't do it."

"You have the strength of will to bond a void beast. What is a shadow? You will do this," he said.

"I suppose," she said, sounding unconvinced. She moved into his blind spot, her features blurring into a mass of color. "Isn't everyone's ability unique? Maybe mine isn't summoning shadows?"

"Everyone has a unique voice, but we all must breathe to speak." It was an old maxim, but true.

"Oh." Recognition rang in her voice.

"Again." He motioned to her to stand at his side, where he could observe.

She stood with her legs apart, one foot in front of another, as if she was expecting an attack. Shaking out her hands, she took a deep breath.

Vekele stepped close, adjusting her stance. He brushed back the red hair from the shell of her adorably round ear and whispered. "You will summon the shadows, and I will reward my mate for her hard work. This is our first bit of privacy in days. I am impatient. Hurry."

She licked her lips. "What kind of reward?"

He chuckled, pressing his lips to the spot where her second eyes should be. "Do not make me wait."

SARAH

She groaned. *That man.* "You expect me to concentrate now?"

"If you are not interested in being rewarded, do not concern yourself." He stepped behind her, his hands on her shoulders. Although she could not see his face, she heard the cocky grin in his voice.

Her arrogant prince. He played her like a fiddle. Of course she was interested. For days now, they never had more than a few moments together before being interrupted. The only time they were truly alone was when he joined her in the shower. It wasn't as fun as it sounded. The shower was way too small for adult fun times.

"You could kiss me right now. We're alone." She gestured to the empty room. "Give me a little sugar for motivation, you know."

"Are we alone?" He placed a hand on the back of her neck. His thumb stroked her skin, sending a shiver down her spine. "Consider security cameras. They may be functional after all this time. Anyone may be lurking around the corner."

"Are you suggesting that Luca is gonna spy on us?"

He leaned in, his lips a breath away from her ear. "When I have you, I do not want an audience."

Her brain short-circuited. Sarah lacked the words to describe how she stood there; mouth open, unable to think of anything beyond his body heat pressed against her back.

"My entire life, I have been on display. For my parents, for the court, the nobles, and my king." His hand squeezed the back of her neck gently, then released. "Draw the shadows to us, Sarah of Earth, because I will claim the kiss you owe me."

Talk about motivation.

She took a shaky breath to steady herself. She could do this. Hell, she'd done it once before. Yes, fear made her unlock this ability. Vekele had been in trouble, and something inside her—not something, the symbiote—reacted to her fear.

She could do that again, with less blind panic and more intention.

Closing her eyes, she recalled the moment the light vanished and how absolute the darkness seemed. She saw through Ghost's eyes. The connection between them crackled with awareness. Ghost had been protective then. Now he was curious.

The thing inside her wanted to swallow the light. She let it.

The air chilled.

"Good," Vekele said in an encouraging tone.

Sarah opened her eyes. The darkness was not as deep as it had been during the attack, but it was enough to hide them from cameras.

Tendrils writhed on the floor around her feet.

"Is that normal?" She picked up a foot, distressed to find the tendril attached to her. She had foot tentacles. That was... interesting.

She shook her foot violently, trying to shake it off.

"I have never seen that," he said.

"You don't have to sound so damn fascinated."

"Void beats have tendrils. It is logical that you also have tendrils."

Yup. Still sounded fascinated.

The tendrils reached upward, brushing against her calves. They were cold to the touch but also insubstantial, like how Vekele's wings felt. Solid and smoke all at the same time.

Huh.

She bent down. A tendril wrapped itself around her arm like an overly enthusiastic handshake. Foot tentacles, huh? They weren't badass wings, but they could be useful if someone tried to grab her again.

As if responding to her thoughts, the tendril tugged on her arm.

No as if, she corrected herself. It responded to her will and could be as solid as she needed.

"I have a superpower," she whispered.

"With time, you will gain control over them," Vekele said. He squatted down to inspect the tendrils. His head tilted to one side, and he reached out a hand. He hesitated. "May I?"

"Go ahead." She was curious what his touch would feel like.

Ticklish. That's what.

Sarah jerked back, giggling. "No, no. Sorry. That tickles."

He dropped his hand away and moved to stand. She placed a foot on his thigh.

"Can they see us on the camera?" she asked.

"No."

"Well, since you're down there," she purred, "how about my reward?"

CHAPTER EIGHTEEN

SARAH

THEY WAITED.

And waited.

Twenty years later, something finally happened.

Just kidding. It was four days. Everyone had a job, and Vekele orchestrated it all. She could see why he had been a military officer before losing part of his sight. Command suited him. He listened to the crew and considered their input before issuing orders. He lacked the sparkling charisma of his brother, but, honestly, Baris had been a bit much. The king had commanded the attention of the entire banquet hall that first night at the palace with a booming voice and an easy laugh.

Vekele, in comparison, was quiet and intense, far more her speed.

Sarah's job, while they waited, was to train with Ghost. By train, they played fetch. Sometimes Ghost retrieved a ball with his mouth. Sometimes he burst into a ball of tendrils and snatched the ball in midair. It was a good trick.

Pitch watched, hopping from perch to perch. Oh, and the station had *perches* built in. Not just exposed beams, but twisting pieces of wood, sanded, and varnished, placed in every room and common space.

Sarah wondered what Pitch thought of her and Ghost, if she was amused by their antics or just tolerated their presence. Ghost, Sarah knew through the bond, adored Pitch, and trotted after her like a dedicated sidekick.

Luca played with her phone and peppered her with questions that she couldn't answer. Why did she ignore the text messages warning her to update her device? If it was vital, why did the device not update itself? Why risk individual error? If the device worked as part of a network, did they link together to create a field to open portals? How many portals were opened?

"It is utterly fascinating that such a primitive device could be capable of opening a wormhole," he said.

"I wish I knew more, but I don't. I'm sorry. I just used my phone to watch cat videos," she said.

"Yes, the saved videos were amusing. I do not understand the recurring image of the female yelling at a cat. Is that sacred for your people?"

Oh, boy. Explaining cat memes was a whole thing she didn't want to get into.

She liked Luca. He had a cheery disposition and was easy to talk to. The other guards were all kick-ass giants with muscles. They were fine, but they didn't talk to her. Not really. Whenever she entered a room, the conversation died and suddenly they all had places to be. Basically, they treated her like Vekele's wife and not like her own person.

Luca never hesitated to explain what he worked on, even if all the tech terms went over her head. It was fascinating watching him take apart a broken device, clean it up, swap out parts, and bring it back to life. It was clear he earned his place in the guard with his skills and his quick mind.

There was an engineer building explosive devices, but she wouldn't let Sarah in the room to watch. She hadn't been able to convince anyone that bomb -building was a skill she should have. Just as well. Shadowing Luca meant she got a chance to familiarize herself with Arcosian tech and not be so clueless when it came to navigating around the station or ship.

Then it happened.

The station's lighting went red.

"What's happening?" Sarah made her way down the corridor, headed to the ship. People rushed by, carrying weapons and strapping on armor.

The bridge was a flurry of activity. Vekele stood in the center, his arms behind his back, a point of calm in the commotion. People shouted their reports.

"A tunnel is opening."

"The engine will require an hour to cool down before forming a new tunnel."

Now was not the time to ogle her man, but he looked good. He wore a fitted coat that made the long, lean lines of his back absolutely delicious.

As if sensing her presence, he glanced over his shoulder at her and winked.

VEKELE

His mate looked lost.

"Prepare to depart the station," he ordered. "This will be over and done with as quickly as possible. I have plans with my mate, and I refuse to let the Starshades spoil them."

There was a pause, his innuendo sinking in. Then the crew hooted and whistled. His mate's face flushed that tantalizing pink.

He steered her toward the captain's chair to sit. "Apologies," he said, leaning in to keep their conversation quiet. "I should not make a crass jest at your expense."

"I think they're stunned that you made a joke," she replied.

"I jest. My sense of humor is one of the many qualities that endear me to you, and I have a recording of you saying as much."

She tilted her face up and pressed a light kiss to his lips. "I said you make me laugh. There's a lot of nuance in that."

Nuance. Bah.

As pleasant as this conversation was, he could not flirt with his mate. He had a brother to rescue.

"Status updates," he barked, stepping behind the captain's chair. He rested a hand on the back. Pitch fluttered down, perching on the other side of the chair back. They framed Sarah like guardians.

"Ready to depart the station."

"Excellent. Do not wait for fanfare to send us off. Go," he said.

The pilot straightened in her seat, her hands flying over the control panel. A subtle lurch was the only indication that they were underway.

"Set a course to intercept," he ordered.

"Estimated intercept in ten minutes, but they will see us coming long before then."

Of course. Nothing could be simple.

"Our arrival is hardly unexpected. Let them see us," Vekele said. He had the superior ship with greater speed and fuel capacity. If the Starshade ship fled, he would be directly behind. "When will they be in weapons range?"

"Three minutes. Weapons online, Your Highness."

"Target the tunnel drive when we are in range." The Starshades were not going anywhere.

"The boarding squad is suiting up," another guard announced.

Vekele should also have been wearing armor, but the ship did not have enough for everyone on board. He had packed in more people than the ship could strictly carry. While there were enough rations and oxygen, he had more bodies than armor and weapons. The crew had scrounged a few pieces from the derelict station. A clever engineer fashioned explosive devices to use when they boarded the Starshade ship.

Cobbled -together armor and homemade weapons. That was the best he had to offer.

No matter. He had faced more formidable foes with fewer resources. By the time he boarded the enemy vessel, the fight would be concluded.

The song of battle took over, a tune so familiar that he did not have to think about his part. He fell into the role with ease, letting the chaos of it swirl around him. He saw the pattern emerge.

The long-range weaponry disabled the Starshade ship. His ship overtook the other and prepared to board. The boarding team jettisoned out an airlock, carrying a heavy lance and torches to pierce the hull and force their way inside.

The second wave of guards boarded the ship. Images of the fight filled a dozen screens.

Vekele growled, his hand clenching the back of the captain's chair. His guards were pinned down in a corridor under heavy fire.

Sarah's hand covered his. She did not offer platitudes, only quiet support.

Updates arrived rapidly.

"We've accessed the ship's controls."

"We have the bridge."

"We've located the king."

"We've apprehended Lady Cassana."

Sarah rose from the chair to face him. "It's over?"

"Almost," he said. "Harol, see to the king."

"Already there," the reply came instantly. Vekele's lips twitched. The medic was too impatient to wait on orders, which was one of the things Vekele liked best about him.

He continued to issue commands. "Secure the Starshade ship. Place the crew in the brig for now. Escort Lady Cassana and Lord Starshade to our ship. We are overdue for a discussion."

The guards confirmed their orders.

He moved to leave the bridge. Sarah followed. He stopped and crossed his arms over his chest.

"I'm coming with you," she said.

"You will not want to see this." He knew what must be done. Blood would flow.

"Don't tell me what I want to see. Those people damn near killed us. I'm coming." Her eyes went dark, the beige skin around her eyes turning gray.

When she mastered her abilities, she would be formidable.

His hand settled on the back of her neck as he brought their foreheads together. Taking a breath, he memorized the moment. The scent of her soap. The puffs of her breath against his skin. The way her hands clutched at the front of his coat.

"Very well but stay back. Soon, this will be over, and I will have nothing to do but lavish you with adoration," he said.

"You'd better." Her tone did not invite discussion.

His bossy mate. How he loved her.

With a sigh, he released her from the hold and stood straight.

He had matters to deal with that could not wait. His aunt and the Starshades had much to answer for.

CHAPTER NINETEEN

SARAH

SARAH AND GHOST trotted after Vekele. She honestly did not expect him to give in. She had a speech prepared about needing closure and seeing justice done. If that didn't sway him, she would lean into needing to understand the nasty side of his world since she was staying.

Staying.

She disliked the idea of never seeing her parents, but she couldn't live without Vekele, Pitch, and Ghost. They were pack, after all.

Ghost agreed. He liked the mother bird with the sharp claws.

They reached the common room in minutes. The space was already packed with people. Every person kneeling on the floor had two guards hovering over them.

Sarah recognized Cassana, Joie, and other faces from the banquet. This must be the Starshade family.

Vekele approached his aunt slowly.

Cassana lifted her chin, defiance in her eyes. "You might as well kill me. Do it quickly."

His fingers twitched. No doubt he wanted to do exactly that. "I will act on the orders of the king."

Where was the king? Before Sarah could ask, voices came from the corridor.

Baris limped in, his face bruised, and his left hand wrapped in bandages. In his arms, he carried a small parcel wrapped in cloth.

Vekele clamped a hand on Baris' shoulder. Then the two men touched foreheads. "Are you well?"

"I will live," Baris said. "They killed him. The karu."

The words rocked Sarah. She touched Ghost to ground herself. Their bond was new, still fragile, but she couldn't imagine how empty she'd feel without him.

Ghost whined, concerned. He didn't like her mood. Neither did she.

Vekele released his brother, shock visible on his face. "That is an unspeakable act. Unforgivable."

Baris lifted a corner of the blanket. Whatever was inside, the sight of it drained the color from Vekele's face.

VEKELE

The karu's body seemed impossibly small. Baris cradled his companion in the makeshift shroud.

Vekele was furious for his brother and for the sacred karu who had been abused and murdered. Pitch echoed his sentiments. He had never seen his brother so defeated. He could not imagine the pain of having his bond severed with Pitch. The loss would leave him hollow.

Pitch dove for Cassana, talons out. The female fell to the floor, huddled to protect her face from the karu's attack. "Help! Get it off me!"

No one seemed particularly inclined to help the woman.

Vekele made a cutting gesture with his hand, and Pitch gave a furious screech.

No. Blood. Suffer.

"I agree, but that is for the king to decide."

With a squawk that very much sounded like a pouting huff, Pitch flew to an exposed beam high above.

"Why was this done?" Vekele asked his aunt.

Cassana lowered her arms. Blood seeped from scratches on her face and forearms. "You know why."

He sighed. "I do not have the patience for this tiresome game. What do you wish to do?" He directed the question to Baris.

"Karu are sacred and protected by law. Killing one is punishable by death. Lady Cassana is already dead. Entertain me," Baris said, his voice cold.

A guard appeared with a chair for Baris. He sat down stiffly, clearly in pain.

Vekele marched down the line of five prisoners. He needed to end this quickly. Baris would not let the medic attend him until this was finished.

"You and your mate murdered my parents. You kept me and my brother as prisoners for years."

"We should have killed you when we killed your parents, but I wanted the heir and the spare. You are welcome," Cassana said.

"This information is known. If you wish to hurt me, try harder."

She sneered up at him, blood streaking her face. "Is your mate happy with a half-blind prince?"

He sighed. "I am disappointed at how dull you are, Aunt. Where is the grand reveal? The gloating over your malicious schemes? Do you not wish to dig in your claws one last time before the king's justice is delivered?"

"The king's justice? Is this the speech you gave my mate when you executed him? My only regret is that I let you live twice."

Twice.

He knew then the answer to the question that haunted him for the last year. "Was it a failed assassination attempt, or did you want to blind me?" he asked.

She spat, blood and spit landing on his boot.

He moved behind her, grabbed a fistful of hair, and pulled her head back to expose her throat. A guard handed him a blade.

Vekele glanced across the room at his mate. Sarah crouched on the floor, arms wrapped around Ghost. Rather than hide her face, she stared at him, eyes open in horror. He wished she was not present to witness what happened next, but it was unavoidable.

"A better male would tell you that this gives him no pleasure." He leaned down, mock -whispering in Cassana's ear. "I am not that male."

The blade sliced cleanly across her throat. She gurgled, thrashed, and eventually stilled.

Vekele released his hold, and she fell to the floor. He turned away, unwilling to meet his mate's eyes.

"Dispose of her out the airlock and clean up that mess. Do not ruin the king's floor," he said, accepting a cloth to clean the blade.

He turned his attention to the Starshades, standing directly in front of the head of the house, Corde. Rasti and Kasim flanked him. Joie kneeled at the end. Her eyes were fixed on the blade.

"What is your judgment for these traitors, Your Highness?" he asked.

SARAH

Baris heaved himself out of the chair. "They thought to torture me. To kill my bonded karu. To break my spirit." Physical and mental exhaustion weighed on him. Sarah could see it in the way he moved, stiff and hurting. "They thought they would bind me to them, but they were wrong."

He stood directly in front of Joie. "They tied themselves to me."

"Baris, please—" Joie's voice was little more than a whisper. Her entire body trembled. Tears rolled down her face. "They made me. I did not want to. I can still be a good mate. Your queen."

The king's face remained expressionless. Perhaps Sarah did not know him well enough to read his mood, but Vekele could. He gasped. "You are not considering such a reckless action."

"I am tired of bloodshed. It is an endless cycle of vendettas. It will not end until one of us shows benevolence or we finally kill one another." Baris considered the four prisoners. "Despite negotiating in bad faith, despite conspiring to attack the palace, killing my subjects—innocent people, despite forcing me to sign the treaty, despite murdering my bonded—" He paused, closed his eyes, and took a moment to regain his composure. "And despite binding myself to this wretched, treacherous house, I will be benevolent."

Joie slumped forward, her head hanging low and muttering thanks.

The older man with gray in his hair stared at the king with absolute hatred.

Sarah had a feeling that despite Baris' intention to end the cycle of vengeance, it wouldn't happen.

"The House of Starshade is confined to their principal planet. Any member of the house is not to leave. If they do so, they face execution," Baris said.

"You cannot do that," the older Starshade man said.

Baris ignored the man's outburst and spoke over him. "To ensure that my benevolent gesture of sparing your lives is not abused and that you remain where you are confined, I will seize every Starshade ship. All of them."

"You have no right!" This time, a younger man spoke.

Joie remained silent. She was, perhaps, the most reasonable person in her family.

"I have every right. I am your king," Baris said.

"You cannot just take our property without cause."

Baris' expression remained neutral. It was fucking disturbing, to be honest.

Sarah tore her eyes away to find Vekele. He grinned, like an owl about to snatch up an unsuspecting mouse. If owls grinned. Look, she was stressed. Owl was the scary bird that her brain supplied. Go with it.

"I am married to Joie," Baris said, his voice cold beyond measure. "As my spouse, we share property. What is mine is hers. Was that not your scheme? Hold me captive until you have an heir? Unfortunately for you, what is her property is also mine. As my queen, she is the highest-ranking member of the House Starshade. Therefore, what is Starshade's is mine. You follow the logic."

"The treaty prevents that," the older man said.

Baris gave a weary sigh, theatrical and a touch too weary. "Which was signed under duress, therefore void. The treaty is useless. If you want to fight in the courts, I am sure the judge will enjoy hearing all about how you hacked off my thumb, carved out my karu's eye—"

His voice broke, and he looked away.

"I am done with this," Baris said. With his back to the male, he raised his hand and made a cutting gesture.

Vekele grabbed the man from behind and slit his throat. Red spilled forth, soaking the man's shirt. His eyes were wide in surprise.

Sarah turned away. She shouldn't have come. Vekele had been right. She didn't want to see this, but she couldn't leave. This was his reality. It wasn't a fairy tale. It was brutal and vicious.

She hoped Baris could make it a kinder world, as Vekele believed.

"Does everyone acknowledge Joie Starshade as the head of House Starshade? Or do you really want to debate the finer legal points? Good? Good," Baris said. "Joie, transfer the fleet access codes to me."

A guard gave Joie a tablet. With shaking hands, she punched in the necessary data. Once completed, Baris took the tablet.

"Five ships. So few?" he asked.

"Your Majesty's last attack on our shipyard crippled our fleet," she said, her gaze cast down.

Baris loomed over the kneeling woman. "Place bands on them and keep them confined," he ordered.

Guards hauled the prisoners to their feet.

"Your Majesty, my king," Joie said. "May I have my father's body? I would inter him in the family crypt."

Baris responded slowly. "Yes, though that is the last boon you may ask of me. Take them away."

The king gestured to his brother and said to Sarah, "Stay with me a moment."

He waited until the guards cleared away the prisoners and the blood. The moment they were alone, he slumped down into a chair.

"I owe you a boon, Sarah Krasinski of Earth," he said.

Sarah opened her mouth to protest, but Baris held up a hand to silence her. Bloodied and bruised, missing a thumb, and he still commanded the room.

"Do not argue. I was already in your debt when you agreed to marry this one," Baris said, absently waving a hand at Vekele.

Vekele responded with a glower. It was so normal. Bizarrely normal. After the horrors she witnessed, the normalcy of his demeanor eased the dread inside her gut.

Fuck. She loved that grumpy bastard.

Ghost nudged her hand.

She loved him, too.

"My schemes put your life in danger. I owe you a debt of honor now. Name your prize," Baris said. "If it is within my power, it is yours. If it is not, I will make it happen."

"I don't know."

"Do you still wish to return to your home?"

"No," she said with absolute certainty. "Earth's not home anymore."

She risked a glance at Vekele, still glowering. That was okay. She knew the truth. He wore an icy mask to hide his feelings from those who would use them against him, but he could not hide from her. He watched her with the intensity of a bird of prey, waiting to swoop down. He was the owl; she was the mouse.

Rubbing her arm, she somehow felt the needles that tattooed her years ago.

She reached for his hand, intertwining their fingers. "This is my home now. I'm staying."

Vekele's expression warmed. "Are you certain?"

She knew what she wanted. "Luca said he could use my phone to reopen the wormhole, but he needs... something technical."

Baris summoned Luca. The man arrived in an instant, out of breath from running. "Your Majesty?"

"The princess' device. Can you open a wormhole with it?"

Luca paled. "No...not by itself. I've determined it operated as a network. However, triangulating the location of anomalies will help me determine the origin point and the, um, correct frequency. It is like a key to unlock the wormhole, if you will."

Baris did not interrupt, which Luca must have interpreted as permission to continue. He explained, "Network satellites and sentry posts, theoretically, still record, but they do not broadcast. The data is there, but I need to manually download it in person. It's labor intensive but fascinating."

Sarah knew what she wanted. It had been a half-formed idea for days now, but the more she thought about who would miss her, the more she realized she couldn't be the only one.

"The thing is, every one of those anomalies is a phone with a person attached," she said, explaining her real concern. "It wasn't just my phone that opened the portal. There are more phones than people on Earth, and we're talking eight billion people. Even if the portals happened to one percent of the population, that's so many people. Lost. Alone. Desperate to go home. And that's not even considering the people left behind, whose loved ones just vanished."

Baris regarded her skeptically. "What is it you want, Sarah?"

"Help me rescue those people and send them home."

"Eight million people," he said in a tone of disbelief.

"Eighty million, actually," Luca said. When Baris tossed him a sharp glare, he added, "Your Majesty."

Correcting the king's math wasn't a choice she would have made, but it was a choice.

"How do you propose to do this?" Baris asked.

"Two methods. One, we look for anomalies. That's how Vekele found me. I was super lucky that he found me, but what about the others? That's how we get the media to spread the word about possible human survivors. It's been a month that they've been on their own, on alien planets. Who knows if the planets are hospitable to humans? Maybe they got lucky, and someone helped them. We need to find them and send them home."

"A search and rescue operation."

"Yes. It's a big ask," she said. "Once we have the data to open a wormhole, we can reuse it, right?" She tossed a look at Luca, who agreed.

"It would take no extra work to reopen the portal," Luca said.

"Even if we can't send people back to Earth, we can offer them refuge," she added.

Baris looked unconvinced. She gave her most winning smile.

He sighed. "Very well. Vekele, you will carry out your mate's mission. Collect the necessary data. Investigate the anomalies. Locate survivors. Take Luca, since this is his doing."

Sarah pumped her fist, keeping her arm close to her torso.

"The survivors will have been on their own for several weeks. They may require medical care," Vekele said.

"Yes, yes. Whatever you feel is necessary. Take the Starshade ship, outfit it accordingly, take my best guards, and spend all my money," Baris said, his tone tired and a little weary. "Now, if you do not mind, the medic has been uncharacteristically patient waiting for me."

He pushed himself out of the chair and limped across the room. Every step betrayed the injuries inflicted on him.

Vekele drew her away, leading her to their cabin. The king's cabin, actually. She supposed they would have to switch cabins now. Somehow, packing their luggage seemed exhausting.

Once the cabin door closed, Vekele placed his hands on her shoulders. He looked at her with a deeply concerned expression on his face. "Is this what you truly want?" he asked.

She reached up, cupping the side of his face. In this light, his complexion wasn't a flat gray. It had a heathery purple undertone. "I really do like your face."

"Sarah, are you well?"

"Yes. I mean, no. Obviously. My brain is buffering what just happened. I'm sure it'll hit me when I'm in the shower or buttering toast. Who knows?" A shower and toast sounded amazing, actually.

"Sarah," Vekele said, grabbing her attention. He sounded as tired as she felt.

"Sorry, I'm exhausted and getting distracted," she said. "Yes, I want to stay. I told you."

"The mission?"

"Yes," she said, not hesitating. "I don't like the idea that there are people out there stranded and possibly hurt. We can do something about it. Something good."

His hand rested on the back of her neck, and their foreheads bumped.

The simple gesture grounded her.

This was home. She would miss her parents and the comforts of Earth. The portal took her from everything she'd known and gave her so much.

This was their story, and they would make it together.

"Then I accept your mission," he said.

EPILOGUE

SARAH

Six Months Later

"If you're certain," Sarah said. Standing outside a stone farmhouse, she shifted from foot to foot, aware of her boots sinking into fresh mud. The sun finally emerged after a rain shower. She always thought country air was supposed to smell sweet, but it smelled like mud.

Ghost sniffed the ground, spinning in a circle to chase an interesting scent. He'd grown, nearly doubling in size. Her monster puppy was a full-fledged monster now.

Donna crossed her arms over her chest, leaning against the doorframe. She watched Ghost warily, but so far, the worst thing Ghost did was splash through a puddle. "Your offer is kind, Princess, but I'm staying."

A large Arcosian man stood behind Donna, then placed a hand on her shoulder. Interior shadows partially hid his face. He made an imposing figure, but Donna relaxed at his touch.

They were scared of her.

In the six months since Sarah's search and rescue mission— or Save the Humans, as she called it— they found nearly two dozen people. The media picked up on the story of "lost humans," which helped locate the first cluster. Half accepted Sarah's offer to come with her and hopefully find a way back to Earth. The other half had already found their place in the alien world and weren't interested in leaving. One man, Bernard, landed on an uninhabited tropical island. Said it was the best vacation he ever had.

"Please, call me Sarah," she said. People insisted on using the title. Honestly, Sarah didn't think she'd ever get used to the strangeness of it. Bad enough the Arcosians used the title. It was downright weird being called Princess by another human. "We both went through a portal."

"You landed with a prince, and I have my farmer." Donna smiled sweetly. "I'm exactly where I want to be."

Hard same.

"Well, you have the comm unit. Don't hesitate to call if you need anything or change your mind," Sarah said.

"I won't, but thank you," she said in a firm tone.

Not one to linger, Sarah waved farewell and trudged through the mud back to the flyer.

Vekele leaned against the flyer, all lean lines, and the grin he gave her was positively disreputable. Pitch flew from a nearby tree to his shoulder.

"The female will remain?" he asked, scratching behind Pitch's head.

"Took offense that I'd even suggested she'd leave."

He looked around, considering the farmstead. "It is a pleasant spot. It is understandable that she wishes to remain."

"Well, you didn't get a look at the handsome farmer," Sarah said, only a little tickled at the disgruntled noise Vekele made. "When do we have to be back on the ship?"

"Whenever we please. It is our ship. They will not leave without us," he answered. "I promised you a present."

"Yes. Give it to me." She held out a hand, flexing her fingers in a gimme motion.

"Get in the flyer."

"Can I drive?"

"No," he said quickly.

One little hiccup with the anti-grav and he'd never let her in the pilot seat since. The flyer was barely off the ground since it was in training mode, so no one was injured. That was the point of training mode.

Ghost jumped in the back, climbing onto the towel she put down to protect the seats. Once everyone was situated, the flyer rose gracefully above the line and headed to the west.

Today they were on a smaller planet that inhabited the zone between the inner core worlds and the outer realm. Agriculture was the main industry. Lush fields rolled by. The occasional building dotted the landscape, but they were deep in the heart of nothing. They flew past the last village an hour ago and calling the cluster of buildings a village was generous.

The open landscape went on forever. Sarah couldn't imagine living here. She'd always been a city person. The closest she ever got to a farm was the farmer's market on Saturday mornings.

She tried to read up on every planet they visited. When Vekele told her the Arcosian kingdom held "several worlds," she thought maybe a dozen, two dozen max, and most of them uninhabited.

Nope.

The Arcosian kingdom encompassed a hundred star systems, many of them with multiple inhabited planets and moons, not including orbital stations and deep space stations. Adding to the difficulty was outdated information that skewed star charts and damaged network relays and substations. To download data from monitoring stations that may have recorded an anomaly first required repairing and upgrading the equipment.

It would take years to thoroughly survey the territory, looking for anyone who fell through a portal. At least once the monitoring stations were repaired, they could scan the nearby planets for human life forms.

Reconnecting the communication network helped. As the media spread the story, local reports cropped up of strange aliens appearing out of nothingness. As much as Sarah wanted to scour every moon or tiny planet that could support life, their resources were better spent tracking down reported sightings. She worried about the people that could be alone, injured, or barely surviving in the wilderness.

They needed a bigger crew. Hell, they needed another team on another ship or two. When the king agreed to her plan, he must have known how impossible the task would be.

Sarah added asking for more resources to her ever - growing to-do list.

The flyer slowed. While a force field shielded the occupants from the wind, it did little about the sound.

"Where are we going?" she shouted.

Vekele shook his head, not even bothering to fight against the noise of the wind.

Before long, they sat on a picnic blanket on a high cliff overlooking a stormy sea. A wall of gray clouds lingered on the horizon. For the moment, they were in the sun and the breeze was pleasant. The remains of a meal surrounded them.

Sarah watched Ghost chase insects in the grass. Well, she and Pitch watched. The karu took to guiding Ghost's behavior, especially when in crowds of people. Currently, Pitch swooped down to herd Ghost away from the cliff's edge.

"I think Pitch considers herself to be Ghost's supervisor," she said.

Vekele hummed before responding, no doubt consulting with Pitch. "More like an exhausted nanny. If there is trouble, he will be in the middle of it."

Sarah smiled, knowing it was true. Her bond with Ghost had grown, and she even had more control over the dark tentacles. Despite his larger size, he hadn't outgrown his puppyish enthusiasm. He tripped over his own paws as often as not.

"This is for you," Vekele said, drawing her attention from the frolicking void beast. "For us."

He held out a flat box to her.

Sarah took the box, unsure of what to expect. Vekele had not been humble or modest in outfitting her with anything he thought she needed. Mentioned that she liked the soft sweater she wore? Boom, she found duplicates of the same sweater in every color in her wardrobe the next day. Asked about moisturizer because the recycled air on the ship dried out her skin and a dozen different jars of face goop, soap, and body lotion arrived before the day was over.

He hadn't been proactive, though. He waited for prompts or clues from her. She hadn't mentioned jewelry. She wasn't a jewelry person.

Opening the box revealed a set of silver claw tips.

"Oh," she said, forcing herself to smile. "They're lovely."

"You are a terrible liar," he said.

He had her there. "Do I need to wear these to a function? Or are we going to someplace fancy?"

He moved to his knees, kneeling before her. Carefully, he placed the claw caps onto the fingers of her left hand. "These are not for the public's eye. They are for us. Alone." His voice grew husky. "It is traditional for an Arcosian female to mark her mate. Typically, she will use her claws. For those who have broken their claws or cannot, they wear these."

The last cap went over her pinky finger. A delicate silver chain threaded them together.

"The tips are sharpened to pierce a male's skin," he said.

Sarah held her hand up to examine the caps. A razor - sharp edge gleamed in the setting sun's light. "Is that what you want me to do?"

"I would be honored to carry your mark, but only if you wish."

The longing in his voice came through loud and clear. On their wedding night, such as it was, he bit her— which left a faint scar— and explained the mate markings. He hadn't mentioned it since, and she sort of forgot. Their days had been nonstop busy for so long. Now that things were finally slowing down, they had more time for sunset picnics and, apparently, ordering a custom set of razor -sharp silver claw caps.

"Where I'm from, we just wear rings. No blood involved," she said, her tone gently teasing.

He made an unimpressed noise. "Rings can be lost or removed. Your mark will be a part of me, always."

She did like the sound of that.

"Will it hurt?" She asked, recalling the sharp sting of his bite and the numbing effect of his salvia on the wound. "My saliva doesn't have cool properties."

"Some, but I am not concerned." He lifted the bottom of the box to reveal a cleaning swab and antiseptic gel.

The planning he put into this moment won Sarah over. She didn't want to hurt Vekele, but this wasn't hurting him out of anger or fear. Right now, with the sunset warm on his face, it was clear that this act meant more than simply cutting into his skin and leaving a mark. It was claiming him, choosing him not because the king thought it politically savvy or because she didn't have any options, but because she wanted *him*. Vekele.

"How do we do this?" she asked.

"The arm is traditional. The upper chest is discreet. The back is seen as a sign of passionate love." He tensed, waiting for her response. His stiff posture told her there was a correct answer, but he wouldn't tell her because of some weird alien logic.

Sarah flexed her fingers, weighing her options. Her prince was a touch vain, denying it as he might. Considering how often he wore sleeveless waistcoats; the arm seemed the best location. "The arm. I want everyone to know that you're mine," she said.

His posture relaxed. She chose the correct answer.

Sarah moved to straddle his lap. His arms went around her waist. Sitting taller than him, he tilted his face back and to the side to watch her.

She pressed her forehead to his in his style of embrace, then followed up with a kiss. Starting sweet and warm, it stretched out, quickly growing hot. His hand crept under her shirt and stroked her lower back. She rocked against him, feeling him hard beneath her.

Sarah pulled away, forcing herself to stay focused and not get distracted by the sexy man under her.

"For the record, I will always choose you," she said, placing her clawed hand on his arm.

She flexed her fingers. With minimal pressure, the claws pierced his skin. Red blood seeped up. She dragged her hand down, clawing through his flesh.

He sucked in his breath. When she was done, he lifted his arm and twisted to inspect her handiwork. A smile spread across his face.

"Did I do it right?"

"It is perfect," he said.

Perfect was nice, but perfect was boring. She didn't need perfection. Besides, they bickered too much to be perfect.

Honest. That felt more like them. They could be themselves with one another, as messy and vulnerable as they were, with no pretense.

She hadn't expected anything that had happened in the last few months. Certainly not falling through a portal or finding love. The intensity of it shocked her, sometimes frightened her, but she never doubted the honesty of it.

Here, on this cliff at sunset, in the arms of her prince, was exactly where she was meant to be.

AFTERWORD

Thank you for reading Vekele and Sarah's story. The world is darker than I normally write. I was aiming for a Cinderella vibe and, as Sarah says, it turned into a certain show about thrones and the games people play. Oops? But the relationship between Vekele and Sarah stayed true to my fluffy and snarky style.

And enjoy the super cute chibi drawing of Vekele and Sarah following the afterword. Art by RV72.

Splintered Shadow is book one in the multi-author series, Shattered Galaxies. Each book starts with the same cell phone glitch that opens a portal, but the stories go every which way. I might be a little biased, but I've read a few, and they're amazing. The books can also be read in any order.

Poppy Rhys approached me with the project more than a year ago, and it sounded so intriguing that I couldn't say no.

Working with the other authors on the project has been a dream. Sometimes with big group projects, it's a mixed bag, but this was a fantastic experience from the start. Samantha Rose kept the project organized. 100% would do again.

Will there be another book in the Splintered Shadow universe? I'm planning on it. Baris had a particularly hard time in the book, and I don't like where I left it with him. He needs his own HEA, I think. Timeframe-wise, I don't know when it'll be on the schedule. I have a few more books I've already committed to writing first. This is the writer's lament: we have more ideas and books we want to write than time to write them.

Until then, would you like the book in audio? Let me know. The more response I get, the fast I'll get it in production.

Also, feel free to join my Facebook group to talk about the book or give me an earful about how I treated Baris. (I feel so guilty!)

https://www.facebook.com/
groups/NanceyCummingsReadersGroup

Let's stay in touch! The best way to do that is to join my newsletter:

https://dl.bookfunnel.com/jektemqay4

If you like pictures of cats, you can also follow me on Instagram and Twitter.

https://twitter.com/NanceyCumms

https://www.instagram.com/author.nancey.
cummings/

And I'm trying to learn how to use Tiktok, but I fear
I'm an old now.

https://www.tiktok.com/@nanceycummingsauthor

SHATTERED GALAXIES

Be sure to read the entire series!

1. Splintered Shadow - Nancey Cummings
2. Ravaged World - Ava Ross
3. Scattered Petals – Jade Waltz
4. Fractured Waves – Samantha Rose
5. Crushed Dominion – Poppy Rhys
6. Broken Song – Harpie Alexa
7. Destroyed Desire – Liz Paffel
8. Jagged Honor – Erin Raegan

https://nanceycummings.com/2022/03/17/shattered-galaxies/

ABOUT THE AUTHOR

Join my newsletter and get a FREE copy of Claimed by the Alien Prince.

Get it at here:

https://dl.bookfunnel.com/jektemqay4

I write fun, flirty and fast stories featuring sassy heroines, out-of-this-world heroes, all

the mischief they can managed and plenty of steamy fun. Hopefully you want to read

them too.

I live in an old house with my husband and a growing collection of cats.

Follow my Facebook reader group for early teasers and whatnots.

https://www.facebook.com/
groups/895051017325998/

ALSO BY NANCEY CUMMINGS

Warlord Bride Index (with Starr Huntress)

Snowed in with the Alien Warlord

Alien Warlord's Passion

Warriors of Sangrin (with Starr Huntress)

Paax

Kalen

Mylomon

Vox

Warlord's Baby

Seeran

Rohn

Jaxar

Havik

Lorran

Ren

A Winter Starr (with Starr Huntress)

Alien Warlord's Miracle

The Alien Reindeer's Bounty

Delivered to the Aliens

Tail and Claw (Celestial Mates)

Have Tail, Will Travel

Pulled by the Tail

Tail, Dark and Handsome

Tattle Tail

Outlaw Planet Mates

Alien's Challenge

Valos of Sonhadra

Blazing

Inferno

Taken for Granite (Khargals of Duras)

Dragons of Wye (with Juno Wells)

Korean's Fire

Ragnar

Alpha Aliens of Fremm

Claimed by the Alien Prince

Bride of the Alien Prince

Alien Warrior's Mate

Alien Rogue's Price

Tattle Tail

RECORDING NOW!

Taken For Granite, Narrated by Christian Stark

Alien's Challenge, Narrated by Nicholas Garland

Printed in Great Britain
by Amazon

21515822R00202